The Vertical Hour

by

David Hare

A SAMUEL FRENCH ACTING EDITION

SAMUEL FRENCH

FOUNDED 1830

NEW YORK HOLLYWOOD LONDON TORONTO

SAMUELFRENCH.COM

ISBN 978-0-573-65130-4   Printed in U.S.A.   #24644

MUSIC USE NOTE

**IMPORTANT BILLING AND CREDIT
REQUIREMENTS**

THE VERTICAL HOUR had it's world premiere at the Music Box Theatre in New York City on November 30th, 2006. It was directed by Sam Mendes, the décor was by Scott Pask. Ann Roth designed the costumes and Brian MacDevitt designed the lighting. The cast was as follows

OLIVER LUCAS . . . . Bill Nighy

NADIA BLYE . . . . Julianne Moore

DENNIS DUTTON . . . . .Dan Bittner

PHILIP LUCAS . . . . Andrew Scott

TERRI SCHOLES . . . . Rutina Wesley

CHARACTERS

Oliver Lucas

Nadia Blye

Dennis Dutton

Philip Lucas

Terri Scholes

"We need, in love, to practice only this : letting each other go. For holding on comes easily; we do not need to learn it."

Rainer Maria Rilke

ACT I

Scene 1

(OLIVER LUCAS, alone. He is English, undemonstrative, casually dressed, in his late 50s.)

OLIVER. I'd known for a long time I was going to have an accident. That's how it felt. The effort of concentration becomes impossible. For so many years you haven't made a mistake. Then you make one. It feels inevitable. You signal right, intending to go left. And you pay the price.

Scene 2

(NADIA BLYE is sitting at the desk in her office She is American, pale, poised in her mid-30s, her style casual. Opposite her is DENNIS DUTTON, in his early 20s, also American. He is unusually dressed for someone of his age, in suit and tie, with floppy hair and trainers.)

NADIA. This is not a bad essay.
DUTTON. Thank you.
NADIA. It's not bad.

(DUTTON waits.)

NADIA. Clearly, I haven't persuaded you to my view of politics.
DUTTON. I know your view.
NADIA. It's competing claims, isn't it? If I had to sum it up.
DUTTON. That's your view.
NADIA. That's right. People want different things. The things they want can't be reconciled. Not everyone can have what they want. So the mediation between the groups, between the interest groups, the groups who want different things, to that process we give the name 'politics'.

(NADIA waits, but there's no reply.)

NADIA. Ultimately, you could say, politics is about the reconciliation of the irreconcilable.
DUTTON. I don't see it that way.
NADIA. No.
DUTTON. For me, politics is about the protection of property and of liberty.
NADIA. Yes, that's what you seem to be saying in this essay.
DUTTON. It is what I'm saying. It's about peoples' rights to live their own lives. It's about absolutes.

(NADIA thinks, considering how to go about this.)

NADIA. Yes. Yes, but there's a problem, isn't there?

DUTTON. Is there?

NADIA. We know for a fact that human life by its nature tends towards unfairness.

DUTTON. Do we know that?

NADIA. So: checks and balances have to be introduced. By human agency. The state, in any system yet proposed by man – be it communism, be it capitalism — has to intervene to balance things out.

DUTTON. I don't accept the term.

NADIA. What term?

DUTTON. 'Capitalism'.

(NADIA frowns.)

NADIA. You don't accept the term?

DUTTON. No.

NADIA. You don't accept it?

DUTTON. No.

NADIA. Meaning? Meaning what?

DUTTON. I don't think there's any such thing.

NADIA. No such thing as capitalism?

DUTTON. Correct.

NADIA. So what name do you give it then? The system we live under today? The system we call 'consumer capitalism', 'liberal democracy' — characterised by political parties and — I don't know — huge corporations, massively powerful industrial and military interests? The system as evolved by the West, by Western democracies? What do you call it?

DUTTON. Life. I call it 'life'.

(NADIA nods slightly.)

NADIA. No offence, but do you think Political Studies was a good choice of subject for you?

DUTTON. My father wanted me to do it.

NADIA. He's important to you?

DUTTON. Very much so. I admire him more than anyone in the world.

(NADIA looks a moment, thoughtful.)

NADIA. It's just...how do I put this?...basic to Political Studies is the notion of comparison.

DUTTON. Sure.

NADIA. We compare.

DUTTON. Sure.

NADIA. That's what we do. We say 'Here's one way at looking at things, now here's another.'

DUTTON. So?

NADIA. Well, such comparison becomes difficult if we start out with the idea that there's only one system - there's only one way.

DUTTON. But there is.

NADIA. Is there?

DUTTON. I know it's inconvenient to ask, but why do you think America has triumphed?

(NADIA is slightly thrown.)

NADIA. Inconvenient? Is 'inconvenient' the word for America's triumph? And I'm not sure I'm going to go with 'triumph' either.

DENNIS. Why not? Why not 'triumph'?

NADIA. Listen. Listen. This is a school. It's not a madrasa. We're not teaching one path. We're teaching many paths. You say you admire liberal democracy. Well, basic to liberal democracy is the idea of free discussion. The free exchange of ideas. Comparison.

DUTTON. You telling me I'm wrong to love America?

NADIA. I'm not.

DUTTON. I'm wrong to love my country?

NADIA. No. I'm not telling you any such thing. I'm telling you not to be blinded by love, that's all. Not to be made stupid by love.

DUTTON. Stupid?

(NADIA, embarrassed, picks up his essay and walks to the other side of the room. DUTTON is seen to pluck up courage.)

DUTTON. The fact is — I haven't wanted to say — I've come here to say this today — it's you I'm in love with.

NADIA. It's me?

DUTTON. I don't eat. I don't sleep. Ever since we met. Ever since — you must have noticed.

NADIA. What, that –

DUTTON. I've lost weight alarmingly. Have you noticed?

NADIA. I haven't.

DUTTON. I'm sick. I went to a barbecue on the weekend. The smell repelled me.

(NADIA is lost for a response.)

DUTTON. I think of you all the time. I find the idea of you incredibly exciting. Of who you are.

NADIA. Who I am? Say. If you imagine…For goodness'
sake. Let's be serious! Tell me. Who am I?

DUTTON. This woman out there in the world.

NADIA. What woman?

DUTTON. On television.

(DUTTON immediately holds up a hand.)

DUTTON. All right, that was a foolish thing to say.

NADIA. A tad.

DUTTON. It's not what I meant…

NADIA. You have feelings for me because I've been on
television?

DUTTON. A woman in the world. That's what I mean. A
woman in the world.

(After the shock, NADIA is now angry.)

NADIA. Dennis, Dennis, I have to tell you there are now
quite a lot of women in the world. As you put it. Quite a lot. In
fact, the whole assumption makes me angry. How old are you?

DUTTON. 22.

NADIA. I'm a feminist and what you're saying makes me
angry.

DUTTON. Why?

NADIA. Because the purpose of women taking part, the
purpose of women being intelligent or public or in any way
represented even, the purpose of women talking on television
about international politics is not to turn men on!

(There is a silence. DUTTON is very quiet.)

DUTTON. You didn't know? You had no idea?

(NADIA looks, deciding how to deal with him.)

NADIA. Anyway, mercifully there's a code. There's a code to cover this sort of ridiculous situation.

DUTTON. I know that code. I've actually got a copy here. I think you'll find…

NADIA. It's not necessary. Really. Jesus!

(DUTTON has taken the code out, but NADIA stops him opening it.)

NADIA. So. So, one way or another, this is our last class together…

DUTTON. Why do you think I spoke?

NADIA. I'm going to ignore what you said. I'm going to forget it.

(There is a brief silence.)

DUTTON. Can I say something?

NADIA. If it's about politics, yes.

DUTTON. It's all nonsense, isn't it?

NADIA. I don't know what's nonsense. You tell me.

DUTTON. The study of international relations.

NADIA. In what way is it nonsense, Dennis?

DUTTON. I took this course — as you know I'm a business major, my interest is start-up — but my father wanted me to broaden my mind. I don't know why. Dad's own mind is about as narrow as it's possible to be.

NADIA. Narrow, how?

DUTTON. He wants money. That's the only thing he wants.

NADIA. Well?

(DUTTON sits forward.)

DUTTON. This is my point : America wins. It always wins. You can do all that historical perspective stuff, you can say it's an empire and like any empire it's going to fall. But not yet it isn't. Not in my lifetime. So. Say there's a runner - the runner wins the race — then the other runners, if they're at all intelligent, they ask 'How did he do that?' They look at the winner, they look at his methods, they analyze, they say 'OK'. And that's the way other countries are going to prosper. They'll prosper by imitating America. And to me that's Political Studies. 'What does America do? And how can anyone else get close?'

NADIA. Well I'm glad my year of teaching hasn't been entirely wasted.

DUTTON. It hasn't been wasted.

NADIA. Good.

DUTTON. In fact…

NADIA. Dennis…

DUTTON. That's what I wanted to say. I didn't want you to think I took this course – well, for any other reason but in order to learn. The last thing I want is to upset you.

NADIA. Thank you.

DUTTON. You're a brilliant teacher.

(NADIA looks wary, fearing what comes next.)

DUTTON. However, we can't — face it — the other thing happened to me.

NADIA. Dennis…

DUTTON. It happened. I can't pretend it didn't.

NADIA. I am not allowing this subject.

DUTTON. I fell in love. In fact, the other day, I might as well tell you, I was talking things over with my fiancée…

NADIA. I'm sorry? Your fiancée? I'm sorry?

(NADIA throws up her hands, exasperated.)

DUTTON. Look, just so you understand…

NADIA. I don't have to understand. In fact, I don't want to understand.

(Now it is DUTTON'S turn to get up, agitated.)

DUTTON. It's not — it's hard — listen! listen! — I don't know if you don't – if you know Maine – anyway, two big families. In our part of the state. Big families. Both – whatever. And for many years, it's been assumed, if you like. Everyone takes it for granted. I will end up with Val. Understand.

NADIA. I just said: I don't want to understand.

DUTTON. But just so you know. So you know the context. Let me say: Val is not just my fiancée, she's also a friend. Val is my best friend.

NADIA. And Val has no problem juggling these two roles?

DUTTON. Val — talking to Val is like talking to someone — someone objective. And it was Val who said, she said 'Look, Dennis, you're suffering. You have been suffering. For a long time. For your own sake, you must speak to her.' It was she who suggested it. Not me.

(NADIA looks at DUTTON, trying to work him out. Then she goes and sits on the far side of the room, as if defeated.)

DUTTON. I wouldn't be saying this. I wouldn't be saying it if it were up to me.

(There is a silence. When NADIA answers she is hesitant.)

DUTTON. What are you thinking?

NADIA. I suppose one imagines – I imagine – the world moves forward. Slowly, the world moves forward. My assumption has always been that society would progress. I work on that assumption. Old attitudes die out. But what can you say? They don't. They don't.

DUTTON. I'm not sure I understand you.

NADIA. As you know, I spend a lot of time in war zones – in Bosnia, in Serbia. In many ways I can only say I prefer it there. I prefer being there because here people –

(NADIA changes tack, not finishing her thought.)

NADIA. Put it another way: I am so far from regarding myself as somebody available to a 22 year-old as not to recognize myself in the description.

DUTTON. But that's good, isn't it? Isn't that a good thing?

NADIA. Let's say, let's just say the self-confidence, the peculiar self-confidence based only on accumulation, on years of accumulation, does not do it for me. I don't confuse being rich with being right.

(There is a silence.)

NADIA. This has been a profoundly depressing few minutes.

(DUTTON looks at her a moment.)

DUTTON. I hear you.

NADIA. Good.

DUTTON. But nothing you say convinces me. As it happens, before I took politics, I took psychology…

NADIA. Oh Christ!

DUTTON. Briefly. Freud.

NADIA. How many weeks? How many weeks did you study Freud?

DUTTON. Three. Intensely.

NADIA. Sure.

DUTTON. Actually you can understand quite a lot in three weeks.

NADIA. You can also misunderstand quite a lot in three weeks.

DUTTON. Do you know this?

NADIA. Try me.

DUTTON. Freud has a theory that we aren't who we claim to be.

NADIA. Really?

DUTTON. Freud says we're all somebody else. Underneath. Underneath.

NADIA. I would have thought that was self-evident. I would have thought that was obvious.

DUTTON. Maybe it is obvious, but have you considered what it means?

NADIA. Clearly, you're going to tell me I haven't.

(DUTTON leans forward, intent.)

DUTTON. Think: The real person — the person concealed — is quite different, has quite different feelings from the person on the surface.

NADIA. Well, it's a highly convenient theory. But that's all it is. A theory.

DUTTON. So what I'm getting at is this : you don't convince me. And something tells me — my own instincts tell me — that underneath you don't even convince yourself.

(NADIA tries not to be angry.)

DUTTON. I think this has happened before. I'm not the first student, am I? I know. I know you won't tell me. But I'm guessing it happens all the time. I don't see how it can't. It must. And yet for some reason you pretend it doesn't.

(NADIA just looks at him.)

DUTTON. I've got a feeling that's part of your attraction.
(This is the last straw for NADIA. She goes to open the door for him to leave.)

NADIA. That's it. That's the end of the course. Here. Here is your essay. And the lesson's over.

DUTTON. Is that it? Are we finished?

NADIA. We're finished.

DUTTON. Thank you very much.

NADIA. No. Thank you.

(NADIA has given him the essay at the door, and now they have shaken hands.)

NADIA. I believe I began by saying politics is about irreconcilable differences. So, by that standard, we've just had a terrific political discussion.

DUTTON. Yes.

(DUTTON waits a moment.)

DUTTON. What are my chances of seeing you again?

NADIA. They're zero.

(DUTTON nods, accepting.)

NADIA. Up until now I would have dismissed you as a sort of throwback, Dennis.

DUTTON. Would you?

NADIA. In all sorts of ways.

DUTTON. I don't see why.

NADIA. You're going into the world of money, is that right? The world of finance.

DUTTON. I'm going into my father's business.

NADIA. Maybe it's my ignorance but I don't believe that world will be different from any other. The most important thing you can take into it is an open mind.

(DUTTON looks at her a moment.)

DUTTON. Why? Why would I want an open mind?

NADIA. Why would you not?

DUTTON. Our enemies don't have open minds.

Scene 3

(NADIA, alone.)

NADIA. It's a choice, isn't it? How you live. How you be-have. You make a choice. At some point in your life you think : there must be an intelligent way to live. And you make your choice. Maybe you don't even remember. Everything conspires to make you forget. But the choice is there. You made it.

Scene 4

(A lawn looking over the Welsh and English countryside. A tree. A blissful, sunny day. There are canvas chairs. The remains of breakfast. Both OLIVER and PHILIP are in shirtsleeves. PHILIP LUCAS is English, in his early 30s, notably hand-some.)

OLIVER. So tell me, tell me a little, so I know something about her before we meet.

PHILIP. Aside from beautiful and brilliant?

OLIVER. Aside from that, yes.

(PHILIP smiles, thinking of her.)

PHILIP. Formidable, certainly. Committed. Articulate. Passionate. Full of strong feeling.

OLIVER. OK. Enough of her faults, now tell me her vir-tues.

PHILIP. Well, the first time I met her she was carrying a book. 'Pas de psychologie, pas de psychose.'

OLIVER. What did that mean?

PHILIP. No psychology, no psychosis.

OLIVER. No, I know what it means. I know what it means. I'm not an idiot. Choosing that book.

PHILIP. All right, Dad.

OLIVER. That's what I'm asking. What did that mean?

(PHILIP thinks a moment.)

PHILIP. Well. As you know, Nadia teaches at Yale…

OLIVER. I know that…

PHILIP. Obviously what she was trying to say is that she isn't keen on the psychological.

OLIVER. I see.

PHILIP. She has a horror of it. I thought : that's refreshing. That's such a refreshing approach.

OLIVER. Why? Why did you think that?

PHILIP. Oh. Because the first thing you notice, it becomes a way of life. People are taught to say 'I think, I feel'. They talk all the time as if there were no such thing as reality.

OLIVER. Really?

PHILIP. Or rather: They know reality exists, they know it's there, but they can't help believing that what they feel about it is somehow more important than reality itself.

OLIVER. You're talking about Americans?

PHILIP. Not only. But obviously. Having spent time there.

OLIVER. It's something you've noticed?

PHILIP. Say you have an experience. Any experience. You're walking along the street and a man drops dead in front of you. And peoples' first response is 'Really? A man dropped dead in the street? How did that make you feel?'

OLIVER. That's funny.

PHILIP. Yeah, but it's decadent isn't it? As if it's not the world, it's not the world you're interested in, it's just your own reaction to it.

(OLIVER looks at him.)

OLIVER. Huh.

PHILIP. I'll give you another example. This is an interesting example. Take the former Yugoslavia, if you remember just a few years ago…

OLIVER. I do remember…

PHILIP. Yugoslavia falling apart, on the verge of collapse. But Nadia told me that before she first went out there, she mentioned to someone 'You know, I think this is really important.' Whereupon the person looked at her and said 'Have you noticed, you seem quite emotional, Nadia? Have you ever stopped and asked yourself why? Why you're so worked up? All this fascination with foreign trouble-spots, have you ever considered there might be a reason? Has it occurred to you, you may just be running away from problems in your own life?'

(PHILIP smiles at the absurdity of the question.)

OLIVER. Well?

PHILIP. Well, what?

OLIVER. How did Nadia reply? Did Nadia have problems?

PHILIP. No, I don't think so. Not that she's told me about.

(They both smile.)

PHILIP. No, on the contrary. Nadia replied : 'I'm not going to Yugoslavia because there's anything wrong with me. I'm going because there's something wrong in Yugoslavia. It's called ethnic cleansing. And it exists.'

(PHILIP laughs.)

PHILIP. It's crazy. It's ridiculous, isn't it?
OLIVER. To be honest, I can't imagine.
PHILIP. Why not?
OLIVER. Because the people who need me so obviously need me.

(NADIA comes out onto the lawn.)

PHILIP. Ah there you are.
OLIVER. Good morning.

(NADIA reaches out a hand.)

NADIA. Hello.
OLIVER. Oliver.
NADIA. I'm sorry, Philip. I overslept. I didn't realize you'd got up.
PHILIP. I got up.
OLIVER. Good. Well this is charming, charming.
NADIA. Good morning.

(NADIA kisses PHILIP. They all stand a moment, embarrassed.)

OLIVER. So. Let me — right — to give you the idea, has anyone explained?

NADIA. No.

OLIVER. This is border country. That way, the sea. That way, the south.

NADIA. Toward the sun.

OLIVER. Precisely.

NADIA. Goodness, I really did oversleep.

PHILIP. It's not like you.

NADIA. It isn't.

PHILIP. You always wake so early.

OLIVER. You drove through the night, so I don't know how much you saw. Philip said you'd only been to England once before.

PHILIP. For a conference.

NADIA. At Chatham House. International relations. It was brief.

(OLIVER smiles formally.)

OLIVER. It's rare as you know for Philip to visit me at all, let alone in company.

NADIA. Actually it was an impulse. It was an impulsive thing.

OLIVER. Whose impulse?

PHILIP. Both of us.

OLIVER. Hence the short notice.

PHILIP. We got cheap tickets.

NADIA. Some of the happiest times we've had together, doing things on the spur of the moment.

PHILIP. Very much so.

(They both smile.)

NADIA. We simply got up one morning and decided we needed a vacation. Please don't read anything into it.

OLIVER. I haven't.

PHILIP. God forbid.

NADIA. Philip and I had both been working very hard.

PHILIP. It's something that happens over there. It's in the culture. You find yourself working every day of the year.

OLIVER. Really?

NADIA. And Philip said it was silly that I'd barely visited the country where he was born.

OLIVER. Or the people he was born to?

NADIA. Those too.

OLIVER. You're meeting both of us?

PHILIP. Yes.

OLIVER. Better and better. The grand tour.

(Again, OLIVER smiles icily.)

OLIVER. I'm being very rude. Let me get you some breakfast.

NADIA. In a moment. Yes. Thank you.

PHILIP. Or shall I do it?

OLIVER. Philip has actually tried to tell me what you do. I can't say I understand it entirely.

PHILIP. Oh, Dad…

OLIVER. What?

PHILIP. For God's sake!

NADIA. I'm not sure I do either.

PHILIP. Putting Nadia on the spot.

OLIVER. I'm not putting her on the spot. I'm making conversation.

PHILIP. That's even worse!

OLIVER. Even: I'm interested.

PHILIP. She's only just got up.

NADIA. I can't believe you want a lecture from me.

OLIVER. I'm not asking for a lecture. I'm asking for enlightenment.

NADIA. OK.

OLIVER. Thank you.

(They all smile. It's easier.)

NADIA. I teach politics. That's what I do. It's what I always wanted to do.

OLIVER. From when you were young?

NADIA. Exactly. In fact, I remember -

OLIVER. Yes?

NADIA. Even at school, I remember being bewildered. So much time spent reading - I don't know - medieval literature, doing trigonometry when meanwhile, all the important things were being ignored.

OLIVER. What were they? What were the important things?

NADIA. All right: the obvious things.

OLIVER. Which are?

NADIA. I don't know. I suppose: Why so many people live in such poverty. And so few live well. And what can we do about it? These huge facts, these enormous facts not up for study. Ignored. You'd think that to be alive would mean to want to find out.

(OLIVER looks at her a moment.)

OLIVER. But specifically...

NADIA. Yes?

OLIVER. Philip had suggested...

NADIA. Yes?

OLIVER. Your area is now international relations?

NADIA. That's right.

OLIVER. Your specific concern.

NADIA. My field.

OLIVER. With a particular interest in terror.

NADIA. Oh, no, not 'particular'.

OLIVER. I read on the internet: you're known as the professor of terror.

PHILIP. That's what she has to put up with.

NADIA. Only in the media. And among a few of my students. The dumber ones.

OLIVER. Do you have stupid students?

NADIA. I'm afraid I do. Or at least I was thinking before I left.

OLIVER. Why? Why before you left?

NADIA. Oh. Something that happened. A student. My God. Made me think.

(NADIA smiles.)

PHILIP. Excuse me. I'm going to get coffee.

(PHILIP goes out.)

OLIVER. But you have written about terror?

NADIA. Of course. Everyone does. You can't do what I do and not be fascinated by it.

(OLIVER waits for her to go on.)

NADIA. All right, crudely, if you're asking, you can say, if you want to put it this way, that terrorism may be the wrong answer to the right question.

OLIVER. What question is that?

NADIA. Well, I'd have thought terror's an attack on modernity, isn't it?

OLIVER. I'm never sure. Tell me what 'modernity' means.

NADIA. Usually it means that human beings feel themselves discontent, they feel lost in the world – if there's nothing but the world - and they imagine that materialism must therefore be at fault.

(NADIA shifts.)

NADIA. Of course – look, not to insult you – it's much more complicated than that...

OLIVER. Of course...

NADIA. And the actual motivation...

OLIVER. Yes...

NADIA. ...the moment at which an individual picks up a gun, or straps on explosives – that moment is still deeply obscure. People claim to understand it, but do they? I certainly don't. But underlying that desire you'll often find the same discontent: namely, the conviction that materialism isn't enough.

OLIVER. And is that what you think?

NADIA. People blame materialism because they feel it doesn't nourish them. And you could say, it's true: materialism, by definition, isn't heroic. People no longer want to do dangerous, outstanding things. In the West, you no longer become famous for what you do, simply for what happens to you. We celebrate victims, not heroes. We're infantilized by fear to a point where all we want is to live as long and comfortably as possible. And so this new Western ethic of survival, simply surviving as a human being – merely surviving – as though the world were everything, and the manner in which you live in it unimportant — seems to other people, other cultures, well… ignoble.

    OLIVER. Do you agree?

    NADIA. Me?

    OLIVER. Is that your own view? Do you feel that?

(NADIA looks at him a moment.)

    NADIA. I don't know. But, whether it is or not, the answer isn't violence.

(PHILIP appears on the lawn.)

    PHILIP. I'm assuming you want toast.

    NADIA. Yes, please.

    PHILIP. Honey or jam?

    NADIA. Honey. No, jam. Honey.

    PHILIP. I'll bring both.

(PHILIP goes. NADIA remembers after he's gone.)

    NADIA. Thanks, babe!

OLIVER. In fact, I must admit when I went to your website...

NADIA. Oh, that...

OLIVER. It lists subjects about which you're available to speak.

NADIA. It's a fancy piece of publicity. Shaming, but you have to do it.

OLIVER. Do you?

NADIA. Sure.

OLIVER. Why's that?

NADIA. Being an academic isn't quite what it was. We find ourselves doing all sorts of things.

OLIVER. I see.

NADIA. Inevitably, yes, I talk to the media.

OLIVER. You make a point of it?

(NADIA looks a moment, detecting criticism.)

NADIA. I was mentioning earlier about privilege? And my special privilege has been to define my job as I go along. The university's been very generous.

OLIVER. You're free?

NADIA. That's it.

OLIVER. Free to do what you choose?

NADIA. More or less.

OLIVER. Because of your status?

NADIA. If you choose to put it like that. I barely teach. A couple of seminars. Mostly, I write.

OLIVER. Philip said there was a book.

NADIA. There is. And I'm writing another. This is a relatively new study. Or rather it's an old study which has been transformed. Am I boring you?

OLIVER. No.

NADIA. You'll let me know if I'm boring you.

OLIVER. You're not.

NADIA. As long as we had two great powers, two super-powers in some sort of balance, then there seemed to be a procedure for determining the world's affairs.

OLIVER. Now there's only one.

NADIA. Exactly. So my area of study becomes more vital.

OLIVER. Especially after Iraq.

NADIA. As you say. Yes. Especially after Iraq.

(NADIA looks again, trying to gauge his agenda. Then she gets up and moves to look out over the hills.)

NADIA. I didn't get much of a look last night but this wasn't what I was expecting.

OLIVER. This spot?

NADIA. Yes.

OLIVER. In what way?

NADIA. I knew you were alone. But still.

OLIVER. I am alone.

NADIA. Is that a choice?

OLIVER. Well, this place would hardly be chance, would it?

NADIA. How do you pronounce it?

OLIVER. Shrewsbury.

(They smile together.)

OLIVER. I came here over ten years ago.

NADIA. As long as that? And you don't mind? You don't mind the isolation?

OLIVER. Philip was already practicing. He'd gone, he'd left home.

NADIA. His mother brought him up?

OLIVER. Officially, yes. But I did my share. You haven't met her yet?

NADIA. No. No, I haven't. He wants me to.

(OLIVER gestures round.)

OLIVER. There aren't many spots left where you can turn three sixty degrees and see barely a single building.

NADIA. You went out of your way?

OLIVER. In France they have this expression. 'France pro-fonde'.

NADIA. I'm embarrassed. I don't speak French.

OLIVER. No? I'm surprised.

NADIA. Why? Why does that surprise you?

OLIVER. Oh. Something Philip said.

NADIA. What was that?

(OLIVER is reluctant.)

NADIA. No, say.

OLIVER. 'Pas de psychologie. Pas de psychose.'

(There is a moment. NADIA seems displeased.)

NADIA. He told you that? Why did he tell you that?

OLIVER. I'm sorry, have I crossed some sort of line?

NADIA. No, no, no.

OLIVER. Please, I didn't mean to upset you.

NADIA. You haven't upset me.

OLIVER. I happened to ask him how you met, that's all.

(NADIA turns away.)

NADIA. It's silly. Why do I want private things to be private?

(PHILIP returns with coffee and toast for NADIA.)

PHILIP. You two all right?

NADIA. We are. Thank you.

OLIVER. Fine.

(NADIA takes her breakfast from him.)

NADIA. Obviously you and your Dad were talking while I was asleep.

PHILIP. Oh, not much.

OLIVER. No, no, no.

PHILIP. Very little, in fact.

OLIVER. Philip's one of those people who's always been at peace with silence.

PHILIP. Silence never bothered me.

OLIVER. If the world can be divided into those who need to speak and those who don't.

PHILIP. People only talk because they're nervous.

OLIVER. It's funny. There's a doctor at the hospital who's notorious for his pauses. Ear, Nose and Throat. 'What are my chances, doctor?' 'Well…'

(OLIVER pauses elaborately.)

OLIVER. If the patient doesn't die of the disease, they die of suspense.

NADIA. And you?

OLIVER. Me?

NADIA. How's your manner?

OLIVER. Oh, reasonably sympathetic, I hope. Early on, they taught me something I try not to forget.

NADIA. What's that?

OLIVER. The definition of a doctor.

NADIA. I've never heard it. Tell me.

OLIVER. A doctor is someone who tells you the truth and stays with you to the end.

(NADIA stops eating and looks directly at him)

OLIVER. Not bad, eh?

NADIA. No. Not bad.

OLIVER. It's pretty good, isn't it?

(PHILIP shifts, not sure what's going on)

PHILIP. Are we going into town? I'd like to show Nadia the town.

(OLIVER takes no notice.)

OLIVER. Nadia's been explaining how things have changed for the academic. The public role.

NADIA. Your father sounds as if he disapproves.

OLIVER. Not at all.

NADIA. As if it were vulgar.

OLIVER. Not vulgar, no. But I have my own idea of what it is to be a professional. The two requirements : to be objective and to be discreet.

NADIA. I'd hope I was both of those.

(OLIVER looks at her a moment.)

OLIVER. Philip mentioned...Philip did mention that the president asked for you.

NADIA. He did. Believe it or not, he did.

OLIVER. You went to the White House?

NADIA. I did.

OLIVER. Goodness.

NADIA. I know.

OLIVER. What did he want?

NADIA. Oh, you can imagine.

OLIVER. Actually, no. I have no idea.

NADIA. He wanted briefing. He wanted advice.

OLIVER. Which you were able to give?

(NADIA doesn't answer.)

OLIVER. About Iraq?

NADIA. Yes. He knew I'd written about Iraq.

OLIVER. Clearly you were in favour? You were in favour of the invasion?

NADIA. The liberation, yes. Yes, I was in favour. I don't think the president would have asked me if I wasn't.

OLIVER. No.

(They both smile.)

NADIA. Whatever you think, whatever your view, I'd have to say, it is undeniably something.

OLIVER. For you?

NADIA. No, I'm not talking personally. I'm talking about entering. Walking in. It's impressive. You're picked up at your hotel in a black car, with blacked-out windows. Five minutes later you're standing on the carpet in the Oval Office.

OLIVER. It's theatre?

NADIA. That's right. Theatre.

(NADIA looks down, slightly embarrassed.)

NADIA. Also in our country, it isn't just the person, it's the office.

OLIVER. He's the president.

NADIA. In America…in America that still means something.

OLIVER. Quite.

NADIA. It really does. Do I sound naïve?

OLIVER. I don't think so.

NADIA. Because from what people tell me, it's not the same here.

OLIVER. Not in the smallest degree.

NADIA. Why is that?

OLIVER. It's hard to explain. But I'm probably typical.

PHILIP. Dad is absolutely typical.

NADIA. How?

(PHILIP smiles, dodging the question.)

PHILIP. I left this country, remember?

OLIVER. No doubt you feel that if your president calls, you have to answer that call. If my prime minister called, I'd let it ring. That's the difference.

PHILIP. It's true.

OLIVER. And what's more, what's more, politics being what it is in this country — i.e. everything, everything — my Prime Minister wouldn't call me in the first place.

PHILIP. That's definitely true.

NADIA. Do you – I don't know how to ask this – am I ridiculous for asking this?

OLIVER. Ask.

NADIA. Does no-one here have any concept of national loyalty? Of being part of a nation?

OLIVER. Oh.

NADIA. Well?

OLIVER. I don't know how to answer. Like most people, I do have a button marked 'patriotism'. But — let's say — I'm choosy about who I allow to press it. Certainly not politicians. And certainly not the Queen.

NADIA. Who then?

OLIVER. Oh you know. Blake. Wilfred Owen.

PHILIP. They're poets.

OLIVER. I know.

(There's a silence. Nobody moves.)

OLIVER. An appeal to patriotism is a contradiction in terms. Especially when made by politicians. You can no more appeal to patriotism than you can appeal to love. You may feel it, but you can't demand it. Wilfred Owen, yes. Fifty seven thousand British casualties on the first morning on the battle of the Somme, sent into a murderous war by the ruthless, out-of-touch political class of the day. People with no direct experience of war, and no knowledge of its reality, send ordinary working men to die on their behalf. They stay at home. The men die. Hello? Hard to explain, impossible to justify. And one man – one great man – adequate to describe the event.

(PHILIP smiles to himself.)

    PHILIP. Dad liked the Sex Pistols as well.
    OLIVER. I admit it.
    PHILIP. Same reason.
    OLIVER. Similar.
    PHILIP. All right…
    OLIVER. Not the same.
    PHILIP. OK.
    OLIVER. Don't make me sound stupid. But I did like the Sex Pistols.

(OLIVER sits back, expansive.)

    OLIVER. The only patriotic outfit still operating in this country is the awkward squad. In the United States, you're building an empire. Remember, we've dismantled one. When Philip was young I remember him saying he'd like to be gay or an immigrant because then he'd belong. He wanted a tribe.
    NADIA. Isn't medicine a tribe?
    OLIVER. Used to be. Now it's freelance. We've been – what's the word? – outsourced. The politicians dismantle communities, then complain that community no longer exists. They

incubate the disease, then profess to be shocked when people catch it. 'Oh, why can't people behave?' Well, why can't they? It's a good question. When the people who make the law become lawless themselves, what can you do? How can politicians lead except by example?

(NADIA smiles, giving up.)

NADIA. You have a high standard.

OLIVER. Not that high.

NADIA. If you're talking about what I think you're talking about.

PHILIP. I don't think there's much doubt, is there?

OLIVER. I don't think there is.

PHILIP. It's a fair chance, one way or another, Dad's returned to the subject of Iraq.

OLIVER. Gosh. How did you know?

PHILIP. He usually does.

OLIVER. 'Usually'?

PHILIP. All right...

OLIVER. I don't think, Philip, you're in a position to say 'usually'.

PHILIP. I agree. I'm not.

OLIVER. 'Usually' when you never see me?

PHILIP. OK...

OLIVER. Not just don't see me, barely ever talk, don't even talk to me.

PHILIP. Whose fault is that?

OLIVER. I know. I'm just saying. For all that.

(An edgy silence. NADIA puts her plate aside.)

NADIA. Good, well, maybe this is the moment to set off for Shrewsbury.

OLIVER. Maybe it is.

(They smile at one another.)

NADIA. Believe me, if it's what you want, I'm happy to have the Iraq discussion.

OLIVER. I'm not asking for it.

NADIA. I'll have it tonight if you want.

OLIVER. I'm not insisting.

NADIA. I've had it every day for the last three years. I never supposed a vacation in England would be a vacation from the argument.

OLIVER. Quite.

NADIA. Why should today be different?

(NADIA gets up and turns, formal.)

NADIA. No doubt, you can imagine, I've taken a huge amount of flak.

OLIVER. I'm sure.

NADIA. In liberal Connecticut defending the war has not been a popular position.

OLIVER. It's not been big in Shropshire either.

NADIA. If you're interested: I was quite clear about why I supported it. I'm also clear about what's gone wrong. And I don't think the mess that's followed invalidates the original decision. I've always supported humane intervention in countries where terrible things are happening. I believe in it. With all my heart. If the choice is between stepping in or staying put and watching dictators let rip, not least against their own people, then I'm for stepping in. I was a reporter before I was as an academic. I've been in these places. I've seen suffering – at ground level. And I've been present in situations in which the West did nothing. I've seen the results of our indifference. So. If you want me to pass my evening defending the right of Western countries to use their muscle to free Arabs from systematic murder, believe me, I'm up for it.

    OLIVER. I'm sure you are.

    NADIA. I take it you were against?

    OLIVER. Passionately.

    NADIA. From the beginning?

    OLIVER. Let's just say, I knew who the surgeon was going to be, so I had fair idea what the operation would look like.

(OLIVER gets up.)

    OLIVER. Please. Don't take it amiss. I'm not being rude.

    NADIA. I know that.

    OLIVER. Least of all to you, to you of all people, Nadia. I'm thrilled my son has brought somebody home. Even if it isn't home. In the proper sense.

(There's a moment. OLIVER speaks quietly.)

    OLIVER. All I want is Philip's happiness.

    NADIA. We want the same thing.

    OLIVER. And if you can contribute to that happiness, then believe me nobody could be more welcome.

(There's a brief silence.)

NADIA. However.
OLIVER. I'm sorry?
NADIA. I sense a 'however'.
OLIVER. No. There is no 'however'.

(They look at each other a moment.)
NADIA. Excuse me. I'll get my things.

(She goes off into the house. PHILIP moves away, OLIVER doesn't move. A few moments go by.)

PHILIP. Can I just say: this is an act of trust. I trusted you!

OLIVER. Well?

PHILIP. Dad, I didn't have to do this. I did it because I wanted to.

OLIVER. So?

(There is a silence. OLIVER says nothing.)

PHILIP. It's my own fault. I have this ridiculous need for family.

OLIVER. Why ridiculous?

PHILIP. Apart from anything, because I'm the only person in my family who has it.

OLIVER. Your mother has it.

(PHILIP throws him a mistrustful look.)

PHILIP. Just look at Nadia. You see what she is! You can tell what she is! This is the best piece of luck in my life! Meeting her! What, I'm not to marry her because you don't approve of her position on   Iraq?

OLIVER. Come on, nobody said that.

PHILIP. Didn't they?

OLIVER. Nobody put it like that.

PHILIP. They didn't need to, did they?

OLIVER. And maybe I wasn't listening but I didn't hear anyone say 'marriage' either.

(PHILIP is silent. OLIVER is amused.)

OLIVER. What am I meant to say? What have I done wrong?

PHILIP. You know full well.

OLIVER. Do I?

PHILIP. You could be a little more welcoming.

OLIVER. Welcoming?

PHILIP. Yes.

OLIVER. Come on, it's been a good old Welsh borders welcome. What was missing? Conjuring tricks?

(But PHILIP has already moved away.)

PHILIP. She said 'I'd be fascinated to see a little family background.' It's not very easy is it? to explain 'Oh you can meet my father, but bear in mind, this is a man who destroyed my mother's life.'

OLIVER. Did I?

PHILIP. And now – for reasons I'm not going into – he lives alone on a hillside, repelling boarders. Or rather, repelling male boarders.

(OLIVER smiles, unperturbed, enjoying himself.)

OLIVER. Philip, this is a tense and unnatural situation.

PHILIP. You could say.

OLIVER. Of course it is. It will test both of our characters to the limit.

PHILIP. Very funny.

OLIVER. Neither of us – all right? – has too much experience of conventional family life.

PHILIP. To put it no higher.

OLIVER. But, in my opinion, I think you're letting it get to you.

(OLIVER sits back, content.)

OLIVER. You say she's the greatest piece of luck in your life.

PHILIP. She is.

OLIVER. In that case, you might ask, why risk your luck by bringing her here to meet me?

PHILIP. I'm beginning to ask that myself.

OLIVER. Well, then, why did you?

(PHILIP just looks at him.)

OLIVER. All right. In fact, take one step back and I think you'll find the whole thing is going remarkably well.

PHILIP. You think so?

OLIVER. She's enjoying my company and relishing the chance to talk to someone who's almost as clever as she is.

PHILIP. You mean as opposed to me?

(OLIVER looks at him reproachfully.)

OLIVER. Look, Philip, if you'd like a piece of advice…

PHILIP. Advice from you?

OLIVER. …then I'd say – just from my experience – I have some experience of this — strategically it wouldn't be very clever when in Nadia's company to show self-doubt. Trust me. It would not be advantageous. Because – I admit, you know her better than I do – but my guess is that Nadia Blye is not someone who easily tolerates weakness. She doesn't like it. Am I right?

(PHILIP doesn't answer.)

OLIVER. Anyone who announces that psychology's a load of rubbish – well, you choose to call that attitude 'refreshing'. I think a better word for it might be 'dangerous'. That's all I'm saying.

PHILIP. You've said enough.

OLIVER. Take one look at her : she's someone who'd have very little trouble attracting any man on campus.

PHILIP. So?

OLIVER. So my guess is, she's picked you out because you appear to be strong. Well then. Be strong. Why disappoint her? As our government instructs us, be alert but not alarmed. Face it: nothing serious is going to go wrong unless you let it go wrong.

(There is a mistrustful silence.)

PHILIP. We're here till tomorrow. We're here till tomorrow night.

OLIVER. Good. Then we'll all take it step by step and see how it goes.

(OLIVER examines his nails, smiling. PHILIP is annoyed with himself.)

PHILIP. And I don't feel self-doubt when I'm in America.

OLIVER. Good.

PHILIP. I like American life.

OLIVER. I'm sure you do.

PHILIP. I like the feel of it. The look. It suits me. In America, I stand with a gin and tonic, I look out of the window, people are going out to the mall and I feel hopeful. Explain that.

OLIVER. I can't.

PHILIP. The landscape moves me. Crazy, isn't it? When there's a road across the desert and nothing in sight. When it snows in New England. Sobbing like a child about a place which isn't even home.

(OLIVER looks down, mischievous.)

OLIVER. Well it's always nice, isn't it? to get away from one's parents.

PHILIP. In my case very much so.

OLIVER. And what's more with an American girl-friend. Though from what I read in the magazines American women can be quite exacting.

(PHILIP turns, half-amused, half-exasperated.)

PHILIP. Oh God, are you off again?

OLIVER. Am I?

PHILIP. Why do you do this? My whole life, you did this stuff. Did nobody tell you? Kids aren't meant to be objects of satire, you know. That's not why most people opt for parenthood.

OLIVER. No you're right.

PHILIP. Most people don't use their children to refine their jokes on.

OLIVER. I know. Absolutely.

PHILIP. Well?

OLIVER. You're right. Of course you're right.

PHILIP. You're 58. It's unbecoming.

OLIVER. I'll stop.

(NADIA returns.)

PHILIP. Good, you're ready. I'll get the car keys.

NADIA. I've got them here.

(NADIA holds them out.)

NADIA. Are you coming with us?

OLIVER. I'm not. You enjoy yourselves.

(NADIA hesitates, about to go.)

NADIA. I was thinking, something about this situation reminds me of J. Paul Getty. Do you know who I mean?

OLIVER. Of course.

NADIA. Richest man in the world. I've always liked him for one thing.

OLIVER. What was that?

NADIA. I read, before he took a girl on their first date, he insisted she submit to a full medical examination by a doctor of his choosing.

(OLIVER and NADIA smile.)

NADIA. Now that's what I call romantic.
OLIVER. Me too.
NADIA. Great start to an evening, isn't it?
OLIVER. And good business for my profession too.
NADIA. Yeah. Yeah, that's what I was thinking.

(The two of them stand, amused by each other.)

NADIA. See you later.
OLIVER. And you.

Scene 5

(OLIVER, alone.)

OLIVER. I used to go to the football when I lived in London. I thought, why's everyone shouting at the referee? He's doing his best. In fact I'm the only fan I know who ever took the referee for a meal. I ran into him as he was leaving the ground – and we fell to talking. I told him I'd liked the way he'd handled things. We went on to a restaurant and I bought him dinner. There's a part of me that likes a well-ordered game.

Scene 6

(The lawn again. The remains of meal. A CD player is on in the house. NADIA, PHILIP and OLIVER have been eating at a table under the stars. It looks enchanted.)

NADIA. It seems so long ago, it seems like such a long time ago. I suppose I wasn't there more than eight months…

THE VERTICAL HOUR

OLIVER. That's all?

NADIA. Probably. But it seems like half a life-time. When we were in Sarajevo.

(There's a moment's silence.)

NADIA. Maybe there was something about my being so young. Most of us were. By the time you've got a family, it's tough, unless your partner's willing to accept you might get a bullet in the throat.

(OLIVER refers to the scene around them.)

OLIVER. You couldn't sit under the stars. You couldn't eat out?

NADIA. You couldn't eat. Most nights I was looped, all of us were.

OLIVER. Looped? What does looped mean?

(There is a sudden silence. She looks at him.)

NADIA. Looped? Looped means drunk.

(Everyone is still, PHILIP watching intently.)

NADIA. You'd go out all day in what we call 'soft skins'…

OLIVER. Say again.

NADIA. I thought it would amuse you, that's why I said it.

OLIVER. All your correspondents' slang.

NADIA. Yeah…

ou're a tribe.

Amm.

K. So, 'soft skin'?

A. 'Soft skin' meaning a car with no armour. An un-armoured car. A regular car.

OLIVER. So you went into Shrewsbury today...

NADIA. Yeah...

OLIVER. In a soft skin.

NADIA. That's right. Only in Sarajevo you felt it, you really felt it, because you knew there was just a thin layer of tin between you and everything outside. Back at the hotel you were sharing rooms, maybe even sleeping on the floor, you had relationships – these were people you're never going to forget.

(PHILIP looks thoughtful, OLIVER notices.)

OLIVER. But you stopped?

NADIA. Oh, yes.

OLIVER. You no longer do it. Why?

NADIA. The whole thing. The anger. I found myself addicted.

OLIVER. Which? To the anger or the way of life?

NADIA. Both.

OLIVER. Anger against what?

NADIA. Anger against the world. The world, for standing by, for knowing and not intervening.

(NADIA shakes her head, remembering.)

NADIA. Endless days, days lying on a floor in a blackout, watching people die for no purpose, for no reason, except the

world's laziness, its fat-spoiled sense of itself, its stupid fascination with handbags and losing body weight and who won the
Open and who takes an iron to the green. Who cares? Who the
fuck cares? The first great war in Europe since 1945 and nobody's able even to remember which country is which. Which
one's Milosevic and which one's the other guy? And which is
Croatia, remind me? Is that the one full of Muslims? Or is that
Bosnia? I mean, who are we? Who the fuck are we?

*(There's a moment's silence. Is she drunk? OLIVER'S gaze is
     steady.)*

NADIA. Three hundred thousand people killed in Europe.

(NADIA shakes her head.)

NADIA. There were nights so cold, so pitted from the trace
of machine gun fire, I didn't know concrete could have so many
holes and still stand. Like lattice-work. There were bodies – every shape, every colour, bodies rotting in the woods, on building sites – ceaseless, pointless violence, dinning in your head
so you wanted to scream. And three hundred miles away there
were people going to the opera and hailing gondolas and laughing, not wanting to know, not needing to know. Because they
didn't believe the war would come anywhere near them.

(OLIVER reaches tactfully for the bottle and refills her glass.)

NADIA. Well, now they have their war, and good luck to
them.
OLIVER. You still feel it.

NADIA. Yes. I feel it. When I've had a few drinks.

(NADIA acknowledges the glass in her hand)

NADIA. Philip's heard it before.
PHILIP. I don't mind.

(PHILIP smiles a little, reassuring.)

NADIA. Forgive me. It's a drug. The anger's a drug. I don't like that part of myself.
OLIVER. You think it's unattractive?
NADIA. I don't give a fuck if it's attractive. I only care what it feels like, and it doesn't feel good.
OLIVER. Because?
NADIA. For the obvious reason.
OLIVER. What's that?
NADIA. What, I'm supposed to spend all my time believing that everyone's wrong except me? The world is uncaring and ignorant except for me? Please!
OLIVER. I understand.
NADIA. No, walking around feeling that all the time doesn't make anyone happy — unless of course they're a psychopath, or – I don't know – one of your poets.

(NADIA stares a moment, the anger unabated.)

OLIVER. And that's the reason you stopped?
NADIA. I went out a reporter. I came back an analyst.
OLIVER. Maybe your temperament was wrong.
NADIA. Maybe.

OLIVER. Psychologically.

(NADIA looks up, sharply. OLIVER smiles.)

OLIVER. To use that word.

NADIA. Look, it was simple. It was a simple thing.

OLIVER. Was it?

NADIA. Yes. Don't make it out to be complex. At the end of it all, when I wasn't plain scared or exhausted, I just felt, shit, I'm spending too much of my time feeling self-righteous.

OLIVER. Why? Why self-righteous?

NADIA. Oh look – whatever — half self-righteous, half confused. 'Oh you're a foreign correspondent. How fascinating!' Well yes, it would be fascinating if anyone took any notice of what we said…

OLIVER. Yes.

NADIA. If anyone listened! If anyone did anything because of what we reported!

(OLIVER waits, tactful.)

OLIVER. But actually you were right. You were right to be angry. Why should you be ashamed? Those people did die. And nobody did care. Why to apologise?

(NADIA looks at him a moment, thoughtful.)

NADIA. People have forgotten. They've forgotten already. All they think about is terrorism. The truth is there was far more terrorism in the 1980s when nobody thought about it than there is today when nobody thinks about anything else. It's just a fact.

(NADIA smiles, relaxing at the irony. She reaches for PHILIP'S hand.)

NADIA. In fact we went – didn't we? we went to a conference...

OLIVER. Where was this?

NADIA. Helsinki.

PHILIP. Helsinki was interesting.

NADIA. Philip came.

PHILIP. Just for fun. I was Mr. Blye.

NADIA. A man got up, very early on, said, 'Nobody in this room is going to die of terrorism. Let's start from there. You're more likely to die from swallowing a wasp than you are from meeting a suicide bomber.'

PHILIP. That's what he said.

NADIA. He didn't make himself popular. Not in that company.

(They both smile at the memory.)

PHILIP. Actually I talked to him later in the bar.

NADIA. You did. I remember.

PHILIP. We had a beer. 'The point of a conference,' he said 'is to be the person who says the stupidest thing.'

(PHILIP smiles, anticipating NADIA.)

PHILIP. All right, maybe he didn't say 'stupid'...

NADIA. Ah well no...

PHILIP. Maybe he said 'provocative'. 'Memorable', I

don't know.

NADIA. 'Memorable', 'stupid' - there is a difference.

PHILIP. Anyway, we know what he meant. He said, 'That's intellectual life in the West'. He was Egyptian. 'That way you make a reputation,' he said. 'It's a game.'

(NADIA is looking disapproving.)

PHILIP. It's not what I think, sweet one, it's just what he said.

(NADIA laughs, forgiving PHILIP.)

NADIA. It's funny. It was a funny weekend to begin with. I made this stupid mistake...

PHILIP. I didn't mind.

NADIA. I've promised Philip I'll never do it again.

PHILIP. It's just those people. They have no idea.

OLIVER. Which people?

NADIA. I happened to mention to someone what Philip did for a living.

PHILIP. Yeah.

NADIA. Well...

PHILIP. Who'd have thought so many intellectuals had such bad backs?

NADIA. And such a poor idea of how to behave. Not a single one of them didn't sneak up to Philip at some point in the weekend.

(NADIA is gathering pace, excited.)
NADIA. People – can I say this? —

PHILIP. Sure…

NADIA. They have this idea of physical therapy as if it were some kind of trade. As if it were plumbing. They treat him as if he's some kind of natural resource.

PHILIP. It's ignorance.

NADIA. I'd never met a physical therapist till I met Philip, but even I knew they're not the kind of people you press sweaty bills into their hands. In fact, I tell you, there was one woman there…

(PHILIP rolls his eyes.)

PHILIP. Oh Jesus!

NADIA. Well it's what happened…

PHILIP. Nadia doesn't care for my female clients anyway.

NADIA. I don't think that's true. I don't think that's true at all.

PHILIP. Don't you?

NADIA. No. As a matter of fact, I don't. And I don't know why you say it. I really don't.

PHILIP. All right, let's say – how do I put this –

NADIA. I don't know. How will you put this?

PHILIP. All right. At the best of times, Nadia distrusts my female clients of a certain age, of a certain appearance…

NADIA. Some of them aren't in quite as much pain as they pretend.

(It's badinage, but it's spiked. OLIVER observes closely.)

PHILIP. Anyway, one way or another, this woman's Italian.

NADIA. Attractive.

PHILIP. Sort of good-looking. Full-figured.

NADIA. Expert on early jihad.

PHILIP. She says, 'Can you possibly just pop up to my room and attend to my grinding discs?'

(PHILIP raises his voice to pre-empt their reaction.)

PHILIP. I would like to say, can I just say, this woman is one of the foremost academics in Italy? One of the cleverest women in Italy.

OLIVER. What did you say?

PHILIP. I said, listen, signora, as a matter of fact, you may not believe this but in the United States of America, I get two hundred and fifty dollars an hour for what I do. And I deserve it. And anyway I'm on vacation, learning about the pathology of terrorism.

OLIVER. What did she say? What did she say to that?

PHILIP. I think she was surprised.

(He grins, but NADIA is already continuing.)

NADIA. I'd already gotten the hang of this fucking woman.

PHILIP. You'd taken against her. Big-time.

NADIA. Oh forgive me, but she was one of those self-hating liberals.

OLIVER. Oh, one of those.

NADIA. 'It's our fault. They're right to hate us. If I were them, I'd hate us too.' You know the type.

OLIVER. I do.

NADIA. It's dressed up. It comes all wrapped up in fancy talk, but underneath.

(NADIA puts up a hand to forestall him.)

NADIA. Be clear: if what people are saying is that it's our duty to try and understand things from the other point of view, if we have to understand our enemies, then – believe me — I'm with them. 100 per cent. But.

OLIVER. But?

(OLIVER waits. NADIA doesn't want to spell it out. She sips her wine.)

OLIVER. But?

NADIA. But that doesn't mean forgetting what we believe in. Does it? We believe in something. We stand for something too. Don't we?

(NADIA is appealing directly to OLIVER. PHILIP shrugs.)

PHILIP. I don't know. I really don't know. Maybe she just had a bad back.

NADIA. Maybe.

PHILIP. The fact is, in America, it's true, I do all sorts of things which aren't strictly medical.

OLIVER. What sorts of things?

PHILIP. More, well, what people want.

OLIVER. What they want?

PHILIP. It's not strict medical practice. It's not orthodox medicine.

OLIVER. What are you saying?

PHILIP. You have to understand: In the States they're really keen about fitness.

OLIVER. Fitness?

PHILIP. You must know that. Fitness is seen as a vital component of health. That's what my clinics offer.

OLIVER. Clinics?

PHILIP. Sure.

OLIVER. I thought you had one. One clinic.

PHILIP. I did. I did have one. Didn't I tell you?

NADIA. Now Philip has three.

OLIVER. Three?

NADIA. Three, and counting. He's doing really well.

(NADIA grins, provocative. OLIVER throws her an uncharitable look.)

PHILIP. Anyway, there's a fine line between formal physiotherapy and – I don't know – providing the client with a general sense of wellbeing.

OLIVER. What does that mean?

PHILIP. I've just explained what it means.

OLIVER. It's not strict medical practice, you say. It's not orthodox medicine. Well, then, what is it? What do you offer? Give me an example. Beyond physiotherapy?

PHILIP. All right, I have various people on the staff.

OLIVER. People? People of what kind?

PHILIP. Therapists, osteopaths...

NADIA. Personal trainers.

OLIVER. Jesus Christ, what are you saying, do you send people out for a run?

PHILIP. Dad...

OLIVER. I'm asking. I'm asking a question.

PHILIP. What's so special about running? What's so demeaning about running?

OLIVER. Do you go running?

PHILIP. No. Not personally. I don't go running. I employ people. Jesus!

(PHILIP turns away, appealing to NADIA.)

PHILIP. Didn't I warn you? Isn't this what I said?

NADIA. It is, but I don't see why you need to take it so hard.

(NADIA grins, enjoying herself.)

OLIVER. Well I must say, if you want to know what I think…

PHILIP. I can guess what you think.

OLIVER. If you want my opinion, I've done a lot of interesting things with my patients, but I've never taken the fuckers out for a jog. I mean, are you serious?

PHILIP. This is a mistake. I should never have raised the subject.

OLIVER. I'm just saying, putting in all that effort, years of study, education, hard work, and at the end of it all, what are you doing? Handing out those ridiculous little bottles of water and lifting weights?

(PHILIP shakes his head, keeping steady.)

PHILIP. Dad. Dad, you know as well as I do as that there are cultural factors in medicine. You yourself used to teach me.

There is no such thing as pure medicine.

OLIVER. No. But there is such a thing as charging two hundred and fifty bucks to take obese Americans for a spin in the park.

PHILIP. Do you think that's what I do?

OLIVER. And there's a word for it too.

PHILIP. Jesus, do you really think that's what I get up to?

OLIVER. I don't know what you get up to. I'm a doctor, I'm not a personal healer.

PHILIP. They're personal trainers, Dad. Personal trainers, not personal healers.

(NADIA smiles, having a good time.)

PHILIP. Dad, I take on people. Ordinary people. You say 'Tell them the truth and stay with them to the end.' How about 'delay the end?' That's not ignoble is it?

OLIVER. No, it's not.

PHILIP. That's not wrong?

OLIVER. Certainly not.

PHILIP. 'Put off the end.' Why not? Get fit, feel better, sort out your problems.

OLIVER. 'Sort out your problems?' God, don't say you talk to the bastards as well!

PHILIP. Isn't it called preventative medicine, Dad, and wasn't it something we were all brought up to believe in?

OLIVER. Of course.

PHILIP. So?

(PHILIP waits.)

PHILIP. So?

(Still OLIVER says nothing.)

PHILIP. We work to stop you getting ill, rather than treating you when it's too late. What's wrong with that? It's the future of medicine, Dad. Or did nobody tell you? Word not reached you? It's all a damned sight more useful than writing prescriptions for a living.

OLIVER. Don't worry, there's no need to worry about it.

PHILIP. I shan't.

OLIVER. There's no need to be defensive.

PHILIP. I'm not defensive. I'm aggressive. You're living in the past.

OLIVER. It's your business. And it's not as if I have such a high opinion of doctors myself.

NADIA. Why not? What's that based on?

OLIVER. I've met a lot of them, remember?

(OLIVER smiles, convinced.)

OLIVER. If you think you're cleverer than your doctor, you're probably right. A degree in medicine is proof of not very much. It's amazing how many people will feel twelve peaches in the supermarket before choosing the one they want, yet they go to the first doctor without a moment's thought. Nothing depending on it, of course, except their life. 'Sorry, doctor I didn't want to bother you'. I watch them come through my door : the more modest the manner, the more deadly the disease. Cancer in particular being demonstrably linked to a recent upturn in personal fortune. 'Oh Doctor, I had been through a bad time, but recently I was just beginning to feel better...' Wham!

(OLIVER smiles, at ease.)

OLIVER. They look at you all the time as if you could help.

NADIA. Can't you?

OLIVER. Not if they won't help themselves. The first instinct of a sick person is to suspend judgment. Their immediate impulse is very powerful: they want to put themselves in someone else's hands.

NADIA. Is that a bad thing?

OLIVER. When told you're seriously ill, the easiest reaction is to surrender to what you think is authority. When it comes down to it, people would rather gamble than calculate.

NADIA. Well, it's an easy mistake to make, isn't it?

OLIVER. It certainly is.

NADIA. After all, doctors are always telling us that they know things which we don't.

PHILIP. Aren't they just?

OLIVER. The job is to tell the patients everything I can. Then it's up to them.

NADIA. Have you always thought like that?

OLIVER. I'm a GP, remember? Behind me, the ranks of experts, waiting.

NADIA. Did you never want to be an expert yourself?

OLIVER. I was an expert. Long ago.

(There's a silence. They expect him to go on.)

NADIA. What happened?
(OLIVER smiles. Then he reaches for the bottle.)

OLIVER. I'm going to give everyone another glass of wine and then we're going to go to bed.

PHILIP. I'm going to take Nadia up Shep Hill.

OLIVER. Take her up.

(PHILIP waits a moment. Then he gets up, picking up some dishes as he goes.)

PHILIP. I need a jumper.

(PHILIP puts a hand on NADIA'S shoulder, then goes out.)

NADIA. What a gorgeous evening.

OLIVER. Isn't it?

NADIA. What time is it?

OLIVER. Gone twelve.

NADIA. He worships you.

OLIVER. I don't think so.

NADIA. Underneath.

OLIVER. Oh no, not even underneath.

NADIA. All right, 'worships' is the wrong word. But he wants to please you.

OLIVER. Not at all. He wants to get me out of the way.

NADIA. Are you sure?

OLIVER. He wants to forget me. That's why he's here. He's doing his duty. He's not doing anything more. This was never a visit of reconciliation. It's a visit of farewell. I'm enjoying your company, Nadia. But I suspect, whatever happens, I shan't be seeing a lot of you.

(NADIA looks at him a moment.)

NADIA. I'm beginning to see...I'm beginning to under-stand how marked Philip is by his upbringing. He still feels bad he didn't become a doctor.

OLIVER. Do you think so? I'm not sure. He was going to Newcastle to read medicine but he never took up his place. It was at a difficult time. In the family. He said he'd rather do something less ambitious but do it better. Fair enough. Far less gifted people than Philip saw bones.

NADIA. When I met him, in fact, what I liked most was his self-assurance.

OLIVER. On the surface, Philip has wonderfully high self-confidence and very modest self-esteem. It's a combination you find in all the most winning people.

NADIA. Did he inherit that?

OLIVER. I think you can say : on the contrary. Or not from me, anyway. You might say I've suffered from the opposite. Excessive self-esteem and no self-confidence. Hence.

NADIA. Hence? Hence what?

OLIVER. Hence.

(OLIVER is thoughtful a moment.)

OLIVER. Philip looked after his mother after I left. He's hard-wired. That's what he does best.

NADIA. Hard-wired for what?

OLIVER. No disrespect, but I think you could say he's drawn to difficult women. They've been a constant in his life.

NADIA. Until now, you mean?

(The two of them are still. It's seductively quiet.)

NADIA. And you?
OLIVER. Self-evidently, yes. I'm drawn to them too.

(PHILIP APPEARS, silently, tense, behind them. Does OLIVER know he's there?)

OLIVER. You'll like Shep Hill. The view is extraordinary. By day they say you can see eight counties. And by night, the panoply of the stars. Weather permitting.

(OLIVER gets up.)

OLIVER. If you hear me in the night, don't worry. I like to read. I like to read outside. I'll clear up tomorrow. Leave it for now. Goodnight. Goodnight, son.

(This last to PHILIP as OLIVER acknowledges him on his way out. There's a few moments' silence.)

NADIA. Well?

(PHILIP doesn't answer.)

NADIA. Is something wrong? Do you still want to go for the walk?
PHILIP. Of course I want to go for the walk.
NADIA. Well then.

(NADIA waits.)
NADIA. I don't understand. Why are you angry?

PHILIP. Because it's an act. It's a mask. You do know that, don't you?

NADIA. Does it matter?

PHILIP. He's not who he claims to be.

NADIA. You mean underneath?

(NADIA smiles at the phrase.)

PHILIP. What's funny? Why do you say 'underneath' like that?

NADIA. Oh. One of my students – something — anyway, this student kept saying : People are different underneath.

PHILIP. Your student's right.

(NADIA waits again.)

NADIA. What's wrong, Philip?

PHILIP. He sits there so fucking reasonable, as if he were the most reasonable man in the world. He drove my mother nuts. Why do you think she was so unhappy? Anything in a skirt he fucks it. He's fucked every woman from here to Akaba.

(PHILIP turns towards her.)

PHILIP. And he killed one as well. Oh by accident, it was an accident. But he killed someone.

NADIA. A patient?

PHILIP. No. Not a patient.

NADIA. Who then?

(PHILIP looks away.)

NADIA. I don't understand. What's up, Philip? This isn't like you.

(Suddenly PHILIP is passionate.)

PHILIP. People aren't their views, you know. They aren't their opinions. They aren't just what they say. They aren't the stuff that comes out of their mouths!

NADIA. I know that.

PHILIP. Urbane! Civilised! It's a trick. Anyone can do that. It bears no relation to who he is. All that high-mindedness! All that principle! The love of literature!

(PHILIP shakes his head in contempt.)

PHILIP. And apart from anything else – I know you won't believe it because it's unbelievable – but he's trying to seduce you.

NADIA. Don't be ridiculous. You dope!

PHILIP. He is. He wants to remove his son's girlfriend and take her to bed.

NADIA. I don't think so, Philip. I don't think it's likely.

PHILIP. That's what he does. That's the sort of thing he does. Throughout my childhood. He smuggled a French prostitute across the Channel in the boot of a car.

(NADIA can't help laughing.)

PHILIP. You think it's funny?

NADIA. I do think it's funny yes. For god's sake. You've

got to escape this stuff.

PHILIP. Oh yes? Have you escaped this stuff?

NADIA. I don't know. I'm searching for any recollection of my father putting hookers in the back of his car.

(PHILIP shakes his head.)

NADIA. And we say trunk. In the States we say trunk.

PHILIP. What about a man who fucks some woman in the living room, while my mother's sleeping upstairs?

NADIA. Did he do that?

PHILIP. Is that funny? Is that charming?

(NADIA concedes.)

NADIA. All right.

PHILIP. Just look back.

NADIA. At what?

PHILIP. At the way the day has gone. Look at it! It began with him undermining. The subtle undermining. Even you must have noticed, the way he set out to subvert you. How he doesn't approve of you going to see the president.

NADIA. Oh, that.

(NADIA smiles to herself.)

PHILIP. How you must have sold out. How you must be some kind of raging opportunist for supporting the war in Iraq. In your own interests, he implied. For reasons of personal ambition, he implied. No integrity, he implied. Well?

(NADIA has no answer.)

PHILIP. Then calculated – I promise you – calculated, not spontaneous: The switch. Oh suddenly he doesn't dislike you. Suddenly, he makes you a meal and he thinks you're great. I've seen him do it so many times. So the woman thinks 'Oh, he's changed towards me. That's interesting. What an interesting man!' God, it's so pathetically obvious. It's Casanova Page One.

NADIA. Why does it matter?

PHILIP. It matters because it's wrong!

(PHILIP moves away in anger.)

PHILIP. And it's disgusting. My whole childhood a trail of women fucked over and spat out while my mother sat alone…

(There's a silence. NADIA speaks quietly.)

NADIA. And you don't think now's the time to start to get over it?

PHILIP. Of course I do. I am over it. I got over it. It doesn't matter to me any more. I'm just pointing it out.

NADIA. Good.

PHILIP. What does 'good' mean?

NADIA. What do you think it means?

(NADIA waits a moment, taking him seriously. She's calm.)

NADIA. Where's your sense of humour? Don't say you've lost it.

PHILIP. I haven't lost it. I've mislaid it. I'll find it again.

NADIA. When? When will you find it?

PHILIP. Soon. I'll find it soon.

(NADIA smiles.)

NADIA. Philip, we came for a couple. I want us to leave as a couple.

PHILIP. Yes, well, that would the definition of a successful weekend.

NADIA. I've been honest with you. I've been in a series of relationships which didn't work. One reason: I was often with volatile men. I told you that. You're not like that. Let's say, after some of my experiences, it was a very attractive quality.

PHILIP. Was?

NADIA. Is. It is a very attractive quality.

(There's a moment's silence. PHILIP speaks without bitter-ness.)

PHILIP. Too difficult for you? Too much trouble for you? This whole thing too much trouble for the veteran of Sarajevo?

NADIA. Just, I don't like to see people suffer over things they can do nothing about.

PHILIP. I thought those were the things in life we have to suffer about.

NADIA. I don't think so. No. I really don't think so.

(PHILIP smiles, conceding.)

NADIA. So. Tell me. What are we going to do on that hill?

PHILIP. What would you like to do on that hill?

NADIA. Good.

(The argument is resolved. They stand in each others' arms.)

END OF ACT ONE

ACT II

Scene 7

(PHILIP, alone.)

PHILIP. Asleep. Fast asleep. And dreaming of childhood. My father, the famous physician. The memory of my mother, sitting on the side of the bed, her hair tumbling over her face. Me, alone in my room, looking up at the sound of her crying, as if the plane to America were already waiting, one day, many years later, to take me away…

Scene 8

(The middle of the night. The lawn. OLIVER is sitting in a dress-ing gown on one of the canvas chairs, reading, a small battery-powered light attached to the book. He does not hear as NADIA comes, sleepy, barefoot, from the direction of the house. She approaches, and he turns.)

OLIVER. Do you know what Richard Nixon said when they took him to the Great Wall of China?

NADIA. No. No, what did Nixon say?

OLIVER. He said 'This is a great wall.'

(NADIA smiles.)

OLIVER. It's awesome, isn't it?

NADIA. Kind of.

OLIVER. What I admire : It's majestic in its simplicity. Of all the reactions a human being could have on being shown a wall, Nixon's is the purest. The most undeniable.

NADIA. Nobody fools Richard Nixon.

OLIVER. Quite.

NADIA. He knows a great wall when he sees one.

OLIVER. I think it may just be the all-time Zen remark of politics.

(NADIA moves forward to look at the stars.)

NADIA. What a night! My God, what a night!

OLIVER. It's beautiful here, isn't it?

NADIA. It's very beautiful.

OLIVER. Aren't I lucky?

(OLIVER smiles to himself.)

OLIVER. I don't think my son will be very happy to wake and find you gone.

NADIA. He won't wake up. He sleeps like a log.

OLIVER. Not you?

(NADIA doesn't answer.)

OLIVER. How can you teach politics?

NADIA. What?

OLIVER. 'This is a great wall'.

NADIA. Oh.

OLIVER. Politicians don't speak words, they use them. How can you take people seriously who use language as an instrument?

NADIA. Language is an instrument. Besides, politics is my life.

OLIVER. Really? Your life is work? No other life but work?

(NADIA doesn't answer.)

NADIA. Did you cook the supper yourself?

OLIVER. Who else?

NADIA. Single-handed?

OLIVER. Did you think I bought it in?

NADIA. How did you do the salad? It was delicious.

OLIVER. Pomegranate seeds. It's a trick. It's a cheap trick.

(NADIA is looking out at the night. OLIVER puts his book aside.)

OLIVER. Politicians only speak to please. Or to pre-empt an argument. Or to fill an uncomfortable silence. 'This is a great wall.' How can you teach that?

NADIA. I'm interested in the art of settling differences. To me, that's what it's about. How do we all get along when we want different things?

OLIVER. Is that what it's about?

NADIA. I think it is.

OLIVER. Nothing nobler than that? Nothing more heroic?

NADIA. There are twice as many people in the world as there were twenty years ago. As more people live closer, their differences become more intense. For the Vietnam peace talks, two months were spent simply deciding the arrangement of the table. The war in Yugoslavia was resolved in the Bob Hope Conference Center in Dayton, Ohio. The session lasted twenty days. But at the end of it, there was peace. It needs determination. It needs resolve. And a measure of honesty. The good people are the negotiators. The bad people are the posturers.

OLIVER. That's the secret, is it? Sitting at the table? Staying at the table? Not leaving?

(NADIA looks at him a moment. Then she shrugs.)

NADIA. Look, I understand the urge people have to turn their backs. Many of us, after all, escaped from Europe…

OLIVER. Your own family?

NADIA. My great-grandparents.

 OLIVER. Where to?

NADIA. Northern California.

OLIVER. Ah…

NADIA. I come from a liberal background.

OLIVER. I guessed.

NADIA. Like your own, I assume. The way you think, the way you speak, they're familiar to me. Public service, public ethics.

OLIVER. Are your parents still alive?

NADIA. Why, yes.

OLIVER. Together?

(NADIA shakes her head.)

NADIA. Anyway — whatever — our first instinct as immigrants was to remove ourselves from your disputatious continent.

OLIVER. Fair enough.

NADIA. That's why we went.

OLIVER. You were right.

NADIA. To get away.

OLIVER. Who can blame you?

NADIA. And if you look at recent American history — World War Two, Korea, Vietnam, the Cold War — then it's hardly surprising, is it? that so many of us are happier within our own borders. What's the point of being rich if you can't enjoy your wealth? When the Soviet Union collapsed, there was to be a dividend. We would live by ourselves, and think about our own lives. But the opposite has happened. We're more and more drawn into the world. Do you wonder so many Americans are in such a bad temper?

(OLIVER smiles.)

OLIVER. You weren't exactly drawn into it, were you?

NADIA. Well…

OLIVER. More like, you stepped into it, don't you think?

NADIA. Depends which part.

OLIVER. Barged in, I'd say. The West's been using Islam as a useful enemy for as long as anyone can remember. 'Shall we go to Constantinople and take the Turk by the beard? Shall we not?' It's from Henry V.

(There is a silence. OLIVER speaks quietly.)

OLIVER. Your feet will get wet. The dew comes early.

(OLIVER'S tone is so private that NADIA turns.)

NADIA. And you? You read all night?

OLIVER. I don't need much sleep. It's a doctor's trick. Snatching sleep on the wards.

NADIA. Everything's a trick to you. You use that word all the time.

OLIVER. Do I?

NADIA. Yes.

OLIVER. I've watched the dawn come up so many times.

(NADIA stands, not moving.)

OLIVER. How was the hill?

NADIA. I'm sorry?

OLIVER. Didn't you go up Shep Hill?

NADIA. Oh yes. It was spectacular.

OLIVER. What did you do up there?

(NADIA hesitates for only a second.)

OLIVER. I'm sorry. What a stupid question.

NADIA. And the view was great.

OLIVER. It is. It always is.

(There's a moment's silence.)

NADIA. Philip...Philip began to tell me about his mother.

OLIVER. Did he?

NADIA. He began to open up. He talks very little about her.

OLIVER. Maybe there's a reason.

(NADIA catches his tone.)

NADIA. It was a bad separation?

OLIVER. You could say.

NADIA. He said agonizing.

OLIVER. It was.

NADIA. She lives in North London? In your old house?

OLIVER. Yes.

NADIA. She never left?

(OLIVER shakes his head.)

OLIVER. Long before I decided to go, there were problems. She'd become obsessed with a need for control. To control life.

NADIA. Her own life?

OLIVER. Certainly. And, by extension, the lives of others.

NADIA. She's a doctor too?

(OLIVER nods.)

NADIA. What do you mean by 'control'?

OLIVER. It took different forms. It's one thing to put a label on the sugar jar saying 'Sugar'. You can put the word 'Tea' on the jar where you keep the tea. But when you type the word

'Fridge' and put it on the fridge, then the signs are that you're in a certain amount of trouble. Easiest to say, her world shrank. From being a woman in the world she became a woman in flight from it. Even the trip to the hospital became unbearable to her.

NADIA. Because?

OLIVER. Oh, the feeling of being seen.

(NADIA waits.)

OLIVER. The feeling of being watched.

NADIA. Was she watched?

OLIVER. Of course not. Nobody gave a damn.

NADIA. Maybe that was the problem?

OLIVER. I don't think so.

NADIA. The feeling of being neglected. Your absences.

(OLIVER thinks a moment.)

OLIVER. Look, you know, plainly it's clear —

NADIA. All right, I shouldn't have said that —

OLIVER. Say what you like.

NADIA. It's none of my business.

OLIVER. Philip has his own view of things, of course he does. His mother's mental state is an issue between us. She's been on medication for a number of years. Philip thinks I'm to blame.

NADIA. He didn't actually say that.

OLIVER. Didn't he? It's no secret. Philip disapproved. Philip disapproved of our marriage. Of the kind of marriage we had.

NADIA. What kind of marriage was that?

OLIVER. The open kind. The kind in which love is free.

(There is a silence. NADIA says nothing.)

OLIVER. Philip's also in flight.
NADIA. Flight from what?
OLIVER. Why, from me. Why did he go to live in America?
NADIA. He's never said that.
OLIVER. No, but you know Philip. It's obvious. Philip defined his life in opposition to mine. England. America. Many partners. One. Pleasure in discourse. Pleasure in silence. I like early Dylan. He prefers late. That's who he is. See it as a kind of strength. He's an interesting chap.

(OLIVER shrugs slightly)

OLIVER. For as long as he could, he tried to keep the peace between me and his mother. Then at a certain point he was forced to choose. I don't hold it against him. He likes me but he'll never trust me. Who's to say he's wrong?

(They look at each other for a moment, level.)

NADIA. Please. I'm not taking sides. I'm simply asking.
OLIVER. It's fine.
NADIA. There's no agenda, there's no motive. I wouldn't have raised the subject but after all.
OLIVER. After all?
NADIA. We're alone on the lawn. There's no-one around.

(OLIVER smiles.)

OLIVER. It was you who said you needed ___ ___ things to stay private.

NADIA. I did.

OLIVER. So? What is it? The night? The night is changing you?

(There's a moment. NADIA looks at him.)

NADIA. In combat medicine, there's this moment, you know, you've probably heard of it — after a disaster, after a shooting — there's this moment, the vertical hour, when you can actually be of some use.

OLIVER. Of use to me?

(OLIVER looks, disbelieving. Then he begins to speak decisively.)

OLIVER. Very well. Our marriage. If you want to know. If you're interested.

NADIA. I am.

OLIVER. I've tried to understand. I've tried to understand what happened between us. Pauline began to suffer from the very thing she most wanted.

NADIA. What was that thing?

OLIVER. Freedom. She suffered from freedom.

(There's a moment. OLIVER waits.)

OLIVER. Pauline said to me, very early on, she said, I remember her saying: "I don't believe human beings need to practise holding on. Holding on is easy. It's letting go we need to learn."

NADIA. Really?

OLIVER. Yes.

NADIA. That's a hard view.

OLIVER. Is it?

NADIA. Certainly.

OLIVER. I don't think so.

NADIA. It's a hard way to live.

OLIVER. Excuse me, but I'm not sure anyone who makes their living as a foreign correspondent is in any position to judge.

NADIA. Why not?

OLIVER. What, rushing abroad to dangerous places?

NADIA. It isn't that simple.

OLIVER. Isn't it?

NADIA. Are you telling me I'm running away?

OLIVER. I didn't say that.

NADIA. Well what?

OLIVER. All I'm saying: you didn't choose the most obvious way of life for someone who wants to invest everything in another human being.

NADIA. Maybe, but I gave it up, remember?

(He looks a moment, but NADIA doesn't go on.)

OLIVER. All right. So. Pauline arrived in my bed with no intention of staying there. We were carefree. We worked day and night.

NADIA. You worked in a hospital?

OLIVER. Yes.

NADIA. That's when you were a specialist?

OLIVER. Training. Training to be. Pauline was living in a certain way — we were medical students, we grew up in the sixties. For God's sake, the body's our field. If you've ever worried what a doctor is thinking when he asks you to take your clothes off, you needn't worry any more. I can tell you the answer. Never underestimate the medical professional's capacity for filthy-mindedness. Pauline had no intention of changing just because she'd met me. You may not believe this, but people of that age, we had an idea. Underneath all the bullshit, all the evasion, all the "I'll see you tomorrow" when you mean you won't — ever — you'd cross the road if you so much as saw the other person coming — we actually had an idea.

NADIA. What kind of idea?

OLIVER. We believed.

NADIA. What did you believe?

OLIVER. Oh. The more people you sleep with, the more you learn.

(There's a silence. OLIVER is quiet.)

OLIVER. The liberation of Eros. All right, it's no longer a fashionable point of view.

NADIA. You could say.

OLIVER. It went the way of smoking. But that's what we thought. The more widely you love, the wider your capacity for love becomes.

NADIA. Did you really believe that?

OLIVER. It was a different time.

NADIA. It certainly was.

OLIVER. Love's a feeling, isn't it? It's a feeling. It isn't the truth.

NADIA. Is it?

(There's a silence.)

NADIA. Go on.

OLIVER. There was a lot of talk about ownership. About not being owned. People not being property. William Blake to his wife: "If you wish my happiness, how can you not wish me happy with someone else?"

(NADIA grins.)

NADIA. They're handy, these poets of yours, aren't they?

OLIVER. Well they are.

NADIA. Never really on your own, are you?

OLIVER. Not really.

NADIA. You always have a poet around.

(NADIA shakes her head, disbelieving.)

NADIA. I must say, it does take a particular gift, it takes a particular flair — you sleep with a lot of women and somehow you want to claim it means something?

OLIVER. Well?

NADIA. I have to ask, this 'generation' you talk about – you think it was time well spent, do you, dreaming up a philosophy to justify what anyone else would have known was simple selfishness?

OLIVER. I think it may go a little deeper than that.

NADIA. Do you? What's the idea? You sleep with a lot of people and it's an ideal?

OLIVER. Well, so it was.

NADIA. I mean, the obvious que
'em for fun?

OLIVER. All right…

NADIA. That's what the rest of us uo.

(There is a moment's silence.)

NADIA. Did do. Did do.

OLIVER. Before you met Philip.

NADIA. Right.

(NADIA smiles, acknowledging the slip. She makes a gesture of 'What can you do?'.)

OLIVER. You may be right. Though it didn't feel like that at the time. For a start, we were a lot happier than our parents.

NADIA. Isn't everyone?

(OLIVER smiles, acknowledging the truth.)

OLIVER. As time went by, I admit, there was a burden of guilt.

NADIA. Specifically?

OLIVER. The ending of the relationship was, for one reason or another, spectacular. Has Philip never said?

(NADIA shakes her head.)

OLIVER. But also the more general question: Could I have made this woman less unhappy?

NADIA. Could you?
OLIVER. How can you tell? I'm nearly sixty.
NADIA. Does that make a difference?
OLIVER. I've learnt a little respect for mystery.

(OLIVER smiles.)

OLIVER. The fashion now is to attack Freud. He's not acceptable, is he?
NADIA. Freud?
OLIVER. Not any more.
NADIA. I don't know. Isn't he?
OLIVER. But there he is, working away, trying to define the impossible line between what we need to suffer and what we don't. We can try to understand each other, we have to, it's our life's work, but finally, Freud comes to us and reports that people remain unknowable. It's strange, isn't it? it's typical that we're all so keen to dismiss this man — 'a prisoner of his time', we say — but in their resentment, their determination he should be obsolete, nobody sees, nobody remembers : there's something beautiful about what Freud's telling us. So many scientists leave the world diminished. He leaves it enlarged. He doesn't explain life. Rather he warns us to take care because so much is inexplicable.

(OLIVER smiles.)

NADIA. Is that his message?
OLIVER. Among others.
NADIA. I've never really known.
OLIVER. You don't approve?

NADIA. Not that. More : one of my student

OLIVER. Yes?

NADIA. ... brought Freud up – only the othe

OLIVER. And?

NADIA. And I did notice, it did occur to me, people usually talk about Freud when they want to get their own way. They talk about Freud because they don't like the look of the facts.

OLIVER. You mean they use him because he's convenient?

NADIA. Exactly. That's exactly what I mean.

OLIVER. In what way?

NADIA. "I don't want to fuck you." "Oh yes you do. Underneath."

(They both smile.)

NADIA. Freud's used to justify everything, isn't he? 'It's not my fault. It was my mother.' Hear the word 'Freud' and it's like a flag. You know there's an excuse coming. I mean, wouldn't it be refreshing to restore the notion of bad behaviour? And people being responsible for what they do? You do something wrong, you own up, you pay the price! Wouldn't that be refreshing!

OLIVER. Goodness.

NADIA. I know.

OLIVER. Well, goodness.

(OLIVER smiles. NADIA stands, slightly taken aback by her own outburst.)

OLIVER. Something tells me you're winding up for a

drink.

NADIA. As a matter of fact, I am. Do you mind?

OLIVER. Not in the slightest.

NADIA. What time is it?

OLIVER. Five.

NADIA. OK.

OLIVER. Five's a good time for a chardonnay.

(NADIA laughs and pours a huge slug from a remaining bottle.)

NADIA. I'm sorry...

OLIVER. No...

NADIA. It's ridiculous.

OLIVER. Not at all.

NADIA. I know I sound harsh...

OLIVER. It doesn't bother me. Nothing bothers me.

NADIA. But I travel in so many countries where all this stuff counts for nothing.

OLIVER. I'm sure.

NADIA. It counts for nothing! It means nothing!

(NADIA has raised her voice, vehement. OLIVER throws an anxious glance to the house.)

NADIA. I don't know, you can't help noticing when you return...when I came back, last time, say, from Iraq...

OLIVER. Is that when you met Philip?

NADIA. Yes.

OLIVER. How long ago?

NADIA. A year. It was a year ago.

(NADIA stands a moment, thinking.)

NADIA. What is it now? Seventy seven journalists already dead, the most dangerous war in the history of my profession.

OLIVER. Your ex-profession.

NADIA. OK. Anyway, this last time I went to observe, not to report. I went as an academic. Not that it matters. They kill you whoever you are. And yes, it's true, I came back to my nice job at Yale, I looked at these kids, looked at my colleagues and I thought 'I know I've got to resist this feeling, I know I've got to fight it, but these people seem spoiled. They seem soft and spoiled.'

(NADIA thinks, then drinks her wine.)

OLIVER. And so we are.

NADIA. As if nothing worried them except their jobs and their bosses and their fucking love-lives. And I remember thinking 'I have no right to despise these people, I have no right to look down on them…'

OLIVER. Nor have you.

NADIA. I remember thinking 'I don't like this feeling. I don't like this feeling at all. I'm not different. I'm the same. I'm not better. Just as confused. Just as lost. Covering up by always having a purpose, always having an intention…

OLIVER. But underneath?

NADIA. Exactly.

(There is a long silence. NADIA shakes her head.)

NADIA. 'Underneath.'

(Suddenly NADIA'S eyes well up with tears. She stands, fighting them back. With no warning at all, she is crying. OLIVER makes the slightest move towards her, but she puts up a hand. Then she goes and pours herself a second, large glass of wine.)

OLIVER. So?

NADIA. So – something I've never done – I went to the gym.

OLIVER. Well, fair enough.

NADIA. The classic response – go to the gym, make minute adjustments to the proportion of body fat to muscle, conform to social norms: Skinny! Skinny! I was in the gym. I was standing there, thinking nothing, or rather just thinking: 'Live a long life! Look as much like other people as possible!' And suddenly there was Philip. Standing near me. Incredibly composed. Strong.

OLIVER. What did you think?

NADIA. I thought 'Here's someone who looks as if he knows who he is.'

(NADIA shakes her head.)

NADIA. Absurd.

OLIVER. Why? Why absurd?

NADIA. I suppose… I'm ashamed to say this. I'm not 16.

OLIVER. It was romantic?

NADIA. Kind of. Yes.

OLIVER. Say it.

NADIA. You're not supposed to like men's looks, are you?

Aren't looks meant to be a sign of shallowness? They say 'He was good-looking, in a shallow sort of way.' They never say 'He was good-looking and it was profound.' They never say that.

(NADIA shrugs.)

NADIA. Oh be clear, it wasn't just his looks…

OLIVER. Of course not.

NADIA. For a start, I liked the idea that he didn't come from my world.

OLIVER. Well, no.

NADIA. He's not bothered by things that bother me. Nothing he couldn't do. Fix a car. My car broke down. Even my roof. He knew what store to go to, he could re-tile a roof. There he was, within hours of our meeting.

OLIVER. Up on your roof?

NADIA. I remember thinking 'I've never met a man like this. A man who can actually do things.' I wanted him.

(OLIVER looks at her thoughtfully.)

NADIA. I'd always associated passion with turbulence. With upset. This was passion, only benign. That's rare. That's very rare.

OLIVER. I imagine, after what you'd been through, it came as a relief.

NADIA. It did.

OLIVER. I'm sure.

NADIA. I might as well tell you, there are so many kinds of men who don't attract me. Include in that: journalists, academics, people who talk about politics all day.

OLIVER. You mean, people like you?

NADIA. Exactly. I've never been attracted to anyone like me.

(They both smile.)

OLIVER. So who does attract you?

NADIA. Oh…

OLIVER. You have the air of someone who's had their heart broken.

NADIA. What makes you say that? Why do you say that?

(OLIVER looks at her, not answering.)

NADIA. Out of the blue, out of the blue, you say that.

(NADIA looks shaken. She stands, waiting for him to explain.)

OLIVER. All right. Last night, when you were talking, when you were talking about your past, about Sarajevo, I couldn't help thinking: this is a woman who's been badly hurt.

NADIA. What, you think you can see right through me?

OLIVER. No.

NADIA. Though, of course, it's not surprising, is it, given your area of expertise? All your background, all your experience…

OLIVER. All right…

NADIA. All your women.

(The mood has changed. NADIA is on the attack.)

NADIA. In fact, would you mind, can I just say something?

OLIVER. Of course.

NADIA. Earlier...

OLIVER. Yes?

NADIA. When you were telling me about your marriage? How difficult it was. How hard to understand. I found myself wondering: You were speaking so tenderly. With such longing. OK, it must be tempting but weren't you rather overdoing the clouds of romantic mystery?

OLIVER. Was I?

NADIA. It's one of those things. One of those gender things. Women's ears tend to get fine-tuned.

OLIVER. Fine-tuned? Fine-tuned to what?

NADIA. Lying. Men who lie.

(NADIA looks, unapologetic.)

NADIA. You made a deal. Didn't you? Isn't that the truth? The two of you made a cynical deal. It suited you. As time went by, it turned out it didn't suit her. She grew out of it. You didn't. Are things really any more complicated than that?

(For the first time she has reached OLIVER. NADIA looks at him, then almost laughs before she moves away. He speaks quietly, to himself.)

OLIVER. I think they are. I don't think that begins to get near it.

NADIA. In fact, I can't believe it, I sat here yesterday, I

was sitting here…

OLIVER. So?

NADIA. Eating my breakfast, you made me feel terrible, you gave me shit about going to see my president…

OLIVER. What shit? I don't remember giving you shit.

NADIA. As if you could judge me! As if somehow you were entitled to judge me!

(Again, NADIA has raised her voice, newly confident of what she wants to say.)

NADIA. The funny thing is, I didn't even mind at the time.

OLIVER. Didn't mind what?

NADIA. My interrogation.

OLIVER. Oh come on! Interrogation!

NADIA. I didn't even notice. At the time I just thought 'Oh this is an Englishman. I've heard about this, this is the kind of guy who sits on his lawn and thinks it's demeaning to get involved in anything.'

OLIVER. Is that me? Is that mean to be a description of me?

NADIA. Charming as hell. But lethal.

(NADIA nods.)

NADIA. But then I woke up. I was lying there in bed. With a nut of resentment. I thought: I'm not cattle. I didn't come here to be examined.

(NADIA looks at him a moment.)

NADIA. If you really want to know, I didn't go to the White House because I was under any illusions.

OLIVER. Of course not.

NADIA. I wasn't going for myself. I went because I thought it was necessary.

OLIVER. Sure.

NADIA. I went because I thought it might be useful. It might be worthwhile.

OLIVER. I'm sure. I'm sure you did.

(NADIA waits.)

NADIA. Well? What's wrong with that?

OLIVER. I didn't say it was wrong.

NADIA. What's the alternative? We just give up, do we?

OLIVER. Of course not.

NADIA. The rest of us give up?

(OLIVER says nothing.)

NADIA. It's easy, isn't it? It's easy, your position?

OLIVER. Do I have a position?

NADIA. Stay home, sit on our hands, look superior, say this administration's nothing but a bunch of seedy alcoholics and crooks?

OLIVER. You said it.

NADIA. Yes, but like it or not, they're the party in power.

OLIVER. Of course.

NADIA. They're the guys.

OLIVER. Of course.

NADIA. And what do we do about the fact that on this one occasion they happened to be right? Whoever they are. Fuck their ideology, fuck their golf-cart morals and their tenth-rate business deals — but I happen to agree with them on one basic thing: it isn't a bad idea when people are suffering — when you're faced with that scale of suffering, you act. You help.

(Again, NADIA has raised her voice. OLIVER looks again to the house.)

OLIVER. All right, no need to jump off a building.
NADIA. I'm not.
OLIVER. Defensive or what?
NADIA. Oh, we're all defensive, aren't we? Don't we both have things to be defensive about?

(OLIVER just looks at her, a little shaken.)

NADIA. Yeah, sure, you're the generation that talked about ideals, have I got that right?
OLIVER. Roughly.
NADIA. Everything had to be an ideal.
OLIVER. So?
NADIA. Everything was a matter of principle! You may have noticed – we are more practical. I admire the practical people. I deal with what's there.

(NADIA nods, bitter, speaking from the heart.)

NADIA. 'Ancient hatreds', that's what they always tell you. In the Balkans I got so tired of hearing that phrase. 'Ancient hatreds'. Whenever people tried to explain what the hell was going on. Oh yes, people love ancient hatreds, because if it's an ancient hatred, what can you do? You don't have to do anything. They tell you all the time in Israel, in Palestine, in Bosnia, in Chechnya, in Ireland 'Oh there's nothing you can do until these crazy people decide to stop killing each other. They like killing each other.' Well it's never true. What is true is that wherever there's a history of violence you can be sure to find unscrupulous politicians looking to exploit it. But underneath there are always rational causes. And 'ancient hatreds' is just the phrase they drag out when they can't be bothered to do anything at all.

(NADIA looks at OLIVER.)

NADIA. It's taken America years, you could say it's taken us centuries to understand that we have responsibilities. Everyone's been begging us 'Take your place in the world'. Then the moment we take it, everyone starts screaming 'Oh no, but you're doing it wrong.'

(NADIA shakes her head.)

NADIA. This was an isolationist government, suspicious of everything that wasn't grubbing for votes and making money. Do you think I haven't paid my price on campus? Kids with four by fours and private trust funds of a hundred thousand dollars a year, coming in Gucci jeans and designer T-shirts saying 'Oh it's a matter of principle. I won't take class with Nadia Blye'.
OLIVER. Has that really happened?
NADIA. Nobody wanted to listen, nobody wanted to hear.

I could have been in foxholes, I could have been shot at by every insurgent on earth – and kids would still come snarling up to me : 'Hey, didn't you go to the White House? Aren't you the woman who spoke to George Bush?'

(NADIA impulsively moves away.)

NADIA. What do you think? What do you think it was like? That day I went to Washington…

OLIVER. I can't imagine.

NADIA. It's true, I walked in that day, I thought this is the oddest thing I've ever done in my life.

OLIVER. I'm sure.

NADIA. Who are these people? What am I doing here? And then you remember it's democracy you're there to defend. Yeah. Freedom. So. In fact, when it comes down to it, there's only one 'principle'. I'll tell you what that principle is : push up your sleeves, put away your personality and get on with the work.

(NADIA is quieter now, her emotion raw.)

NADIA. The only reason you're there, the reason you're talking to the president is that you happen to be an expert on issues exactly like this. And isn't it better to talk to people we have nothing in common with? Isn't that better? Isn't that more useful than just talking to ourselves?

OLIVER. Yes.

(OLIVER smiles.)

OLIVER. Yes, by all means. It's better. Always assuming

people are listening.

    NADIA. Of course.

    OLIVER. It's quite a large assumption. Isn't it?

(NADIA just looks at him. She is apprehensive now, nervous.)

    OLIVER. And you have to consider another possibility, don't you?

    NADIA. What's that? What other possibility?

    OLIVER. It must have occurred to you. I would have thought: don't you have to take care you're not being used?

(NADIA is quiet, no longer fighting him.)

    NADIA. Yes. Of course. I accept that. I know that. Of course I do.

(OLIVER shrugs slightly.)

    OLIVER. After all I don't know what you told the president.

    NADIA. No you don't.

    OLIVER. I wasn't there.

    NADIA. No you weren't.

    OLIVER. I can only guess. I assume it wasn't you who said 'Do it regardless of whether it's legal.' I assume you didn't say 'Drop bombs where you like. Don't take field hospitals, lawyers, sanitary engineers, doctors, or any of the apparatus that any decent, resultant society might actually need. Forget those. Don't take enough troops. Just bomb and hope for the best.' I can't see you saying that.

(OLIVER waits a moment. It is now very quiet.)

OLIVER. I assume you didn't say 'Be sure to have no plan for civil society. Take no notice of international opinion. Manufacture intelligence from the most corrupt and dishonest elements in the country. Sanction torture. Ignore objections. Be deaf to criticism. Somehow magically order will come out of chaos.'

NADIA. No. You're right. I didn't say that.

OLIVER. You didn't say : 'It doesn't matter if tens of thousands of people get killed, just so long as they're not Americans…'

(They both are still, NADIA conceding at last.)

NADIA. Jesus, what a mess.

OLIVER. You could say.

NADIA. We certainly made a mess of it, didn't we? Oh God, I'm so tired.

(NADIA is vulnerable. There are tears in her eyes again.)

NADIA. It's so much easier to do nothing than something.

(OLIVER reaches out a hand. She takes it. There is a silence, he seated, she standing, holding hands. Then, after a while, NADIA shakes her head, and goes and sits down at the abandoned dinner table.)

NADIA. It's true. As you guessed.

OLIVER. What's true?

NADIA. I did have a relationship.

(OLIVER doesn't move.)

NADIA. I did. A journalist. He's Polish. I'd been with him in the Balkans. Then, as luck would have it, who's the first person I meet when I drive into Baghdad? What you might call a hard-line reporter. Meaning: fair chance he's going to get killed. Meaning also: he doesn't give a fuck about anything. As it turns out, including himself.

OLIVER. That's difficult.

NADIA. It is. Or anyone else. Including me.

(NADIA thinks a moment.)

NADIA. Six foot tall. Thin as a rake. A professional. Meaning: he has no opinions. Opinions are for idiots, he says. Oh he gets angry. He gets involved. But it's the job he loves. Dodging bullets. He's unequivocal. He says he couldn't live in the West.

OLIVER. What you're saying is, he's heroic.

NADIA. Yes. Heroic. Heroic. Completely oblivious of his own personal safety. And in the evening...he likes to get drunk.

OLIVER. What's his name?

NADIA. Marek.

(NADIA looks away.)

NADIA. I couldn't take it. He turned me inside out. Like gutting a fish. I'd never known anything like it. I was jealous. Oh, not just ordinary jealous. But wanting to be as alive as he was. So little frightened. I thought: I can't do anything. I can't work, I can't sleep. This will kill me.

(NADIA shakes her head slightly.)

NADIA. Anyway, I came back to America. I met Philip. You'll think me contemptible.
OLIVER. No.
NADIA. I want to tell you something. I shouldn't. You're going to hate me for saying this.
OLIVER. Please.
NADIA. I thought: if I just live quietly with Philip, then I'll get my private life out of the way.

(OLIVER sits back, as if this is what he's been waiting for.)

NADIA. And that's what happened.
OLIVER. I see.
NADIA. It's been very peaceful. I've been at peace. I've gotten on with my work.
OLIVER. That's good.
NADIA. The students don't bother me. The stuff on campus – it doesn't touch me.
OLIVER. Good.
NADIA. Why should it? Philip's always there. He's there when you need him.
OLIVER. Does he know?
NADIA. Oh yes.
OLIVER. About who came before him?
NADIA. Certainly.
OLIVER. He doesn't mind?

(NADIA doesn't answer.)

OLIVER. What I'm asking : he can live with the difference?

(NADIA looks at OLIVER sharply.)

NADIA. He's not second-best. If that's what you mean.
OLIVER. I didn't mean that.
NADIA. Good. He's different. Easier.
OLIVER. And easier's better?

(NADIA hesitates.)

NADIA. I thought so. Yes. I'd begun to think so. Until I
came here.

*(PHILIP appears silently behind them, in night-clothes. He is
very quiet.)*

PHILIP. Here you are.
NADIA. Yes. I was talking to your father.
PHILIP. I can see. I was dreaming. I dreamt you weren't
beside me. Then I woke up.
NADIA. Philip…
PHILIP. It's all right.
NADIA. We were just talking.
PHILIP. What else would you be doing? What time is it?
OLIVER. It isn't yet six.
(PHILIP moves barefoot across the lawn, the two of them

watching.)

PHILIP. It's a beautiful morning.
OLIVER. It is.
PHILIP. Of course that's what you don't get in America.
OLIVER. What's that?
PHILIP. The softness. The softness of the dawn. Nadia's an early riser. So she's already at work when I wake. I look out the window for a moment. It's the only time of day when I do feel nostalgic.

(There is a silence, no-one daring to speak.)

OLIVER. Then what happens?
PHILIP. Oh. I go to make coffee and I cheer up.

(PHILIP turns.)

PHILIP. I'll make some now. Do we all want coffee?
OLIVER. I'll make it. I can make it.

(OLIVER'S beeper sounds.)

NADIA. What's that?
OLIVER. It's probably a customer. I'm on death-watch. A patient of mine. I may have to go anyway. Excuse me.

(OLIVER has got up, and he goes out, taking some dirty dishes with him.)

NADIA. Are you angry?

PHILIP. Why should I be angry?
NADIA. Then good.

(There is another silence.)

NADIA. He hasn't said one single word in any way dis-
loyal to you.
PHILIP. Of course not. He's not stupid.
NADIA. What does that mean?
PHILIP. He has a strategy.

(PHILIP shakes his head slightly.)

PHILIP. I knew you'd get up. I didn't need to look. I knew
you'd go to him.
NADIA. Were you awake?

(PHILIP doesn't answer.)

NADIA. And as it happens, I wasn't looking for him. It
never occurred to me. I simply had jet-lag. I didn't even know
he was outside.
PHILIP. Didn't you?

(There's a silence.)

NADIA. Talk to me, Philip. You use these silences. You
use them against me. Tell me what's wrong.

(PHILIP turns and looks at her.)
PHILIP. He wants you to leave me. I know him. That's

what he wants. He wants to split us up.

NADIA. Why would he want that?

PHILIP. He's jealous.

NADIA. Why is he jealous?

PHILIP. Isn't it obvious?

NADIA. Tell me.

PHILIP. Because we have something he's never had.

(There's a silence. PHILIP looks at her and nods, as if knowing he's right.)

NADIA. And?

PHILIP. And what?

NADIA. And even if that's true, why would I leave you?

(PHILIP doesn't answer.)

NADIA. What possible reason would I have to leave you?

(PHILIP is quiet, regretful.)

PHILIP. I had the idea we were perfectly aligned. When we met. We both have the same way of looking at the world. What you might call, a basically helpful attitude. We'd die rather than say so, but don't we both have this thing about trying to help?

NADIA. So?

PHILIP. It's odd. You've travelled more than I have. You've seen much more. But you still believe the world's all about argument and reason. You're power-blind. It's so obvious: he's trying to exert power over you. It's like there's a dimension missing from the way you look at people. You trust their good intentions.

NADIA. Don't you?

PHILIP. When I read what you write — someone does this, so someone else does that. You simply don't see it, do you? You're an innocent.

NADIA. I'm not an innocent.

(Suddenly PHILIP'S anger begins to show through.)

PHILIP. I was born to an unhappy couple, remember? I woke up every morning, my parents were tearing each other apart. I keep the peace. That's what I'm good at. The conciliator. I've done it all my life.

NADIA. Well?

PHILIP. Until yesterday evening. I warned you against him. I said, be careful. I told you to be careful. You deliberately ignored me.

(OLIVER returns with a tray.)

OLIVER. It's a text message. We're losing her.

NADIA. Who's that?

OLIVER. A patient. I'm losing a patient. It's been clear for a while.

(PHILIP is firm, a new resolution in his manner.)

PHILIP. I was just about to suggest to Nadia it might be nice if we tried to get going.

NADIA. What?

PHILIP. I think we should get going. As we're all up. Why

not?

    OLIVER. Philip...

    NADIA. Can we be practical? Where are you going?

(PHILIP has turned to go out.)

    PHILIP. I'm going to pack.

    NADIA. Pack?

    PHILIP. Yes. Pack. Pack now. I was thinking that way we'll get to see something we wouldn't otherwise see. The road to the Welsh coast is spectacular at this time of day.

(PHILIP has gone. OLIVER is quietly clearing the table of last night's dishes onto the tray. NADIA looks across, hopeless.)

    OLIVER. I'm sorry. I'm not sure how, but I know this must be my fault.

    NADIA. It's so stupid. I can't take it seriously.

    OLIVER. Nevertheless.

(OLIVER waits.)

    NADIA. I should go to him.

    OLIVER. Yes.

(NADIA goes out. NADIA'S voice is heard calling.)

    NADIA. *(Off)* Philip! Philip! Are you really packing? Philip! Do you have any idea of the time?

(OLIVER stands alone. Now dawn has broken, and the sun's

rays are falling across the table. OLIVER looks out for a few moments. Then he dials a number on his mobile phone.)

OLIVER. Yes, it's Doctor Lucas. How's she doing? I see. It's all right. I'll be down soon. I know, but I'd like to.

(OLIVER listens for a moment.)

OLIVER. Please don't concern yourself. It's my job.

(OLIVER clicks the little phone shut. NADIA returns, more amused than upset.)

OLIVER. How is he?
NADIA. Not good. He won't speak to me.
OLIVER. You're joking. Have another.
NADIA. No thanks.

(OLIVER has nodded at the wine bottle.)

NADIA. I will have to go.
OLIVER. I know.
NADIA. It's better.
OLIVER. Yes.

(OLIVER hesitates a moment.)

OLIVER. Before you do…it's true, I was wondering, I was feeling that I'd prefer to have told you. To tell you what happened.
NADIA. You don't have to.

OLIVER. I'd like to.

(OLIVER sits down.)

OLIVER. After all, I'm well aware everyone speculates. I can feel it around me. I've lived here for years but people still whisper.

NADIA. Is this about the person you killed?

(There's another silence.)

OLIVER. Yes. That person. It's what ended my marriage. It was an accident.

NADIA. Well, I hadn't imagined you killed someone deliberately.

OLIVER. No.

(OLIVER hesitates.)

NADIA. Tell me.

OLIVER. Well, you have to understand, I don't know if you know this, the guts are distributed between various specialists. I was a nephrologist. I was very much the man. The man you went to, in that ridiculous snobbish way people have. "Who's best? Who's best for kidneys?" "Oliver Lucas for kidneys." I was very, very rich and conceited. Arrogant, in the way doctors are. I'd been in the country. East Anglia. I was driving back.

NADIA. Had you been drinking?

OLIVER. No. I'd spent an afternoon in bed with a friend. I left about five. I thought if I can be home by supper, I can avoid the inevitable scene. I was on a country road. The man was in

his mid-80s, in one of those — I don't know, we have them in
England – Eastern European cars, incredibly lightweight. Not
even soft skins, no skins. He went straight into me. He never
even saw me. I'd signalled incorrectly.

(OLIVER looks straight at her.)

OLIVER. The police afterwards said it would have made
no difference. It was what they call a 50-50. Yes, I'd signalled
left, intending to go right, but this man was on the wrong side
of the road.

(OLIVER stops a moment, thoughtful.)

OLIVER. You might say, all right, he was going to die any-
way…
NADIA. He was in his eighties.
OLIVER. That's right. Sometimes at the hospital it used to
occur to us we were slaving to save a human being who'd be
dead in two weeks. But that's the contract.
NADIA. What's the contract?
OLIVER. Life at all costs.

(OLIVER looks at NADIA, apparently casual.)

OLIVER. I also killed the woman.
NADIA. What?
OLIVER. Yes. She died at my side. In the crash. I was giv-
ing her a lift back to London.

(There is a silence.)

NADIA. I see.

OLIVER. She was killed instantly. We spun over and I laid her out in the road. Bad luck. She hit her head at an unlucky angle. Very little visible damage. She had a silk scarf round her neck. Soaked in blood. Very shocking. Apart from that, nothing.

NADIA. Who was she?

OLIVER. I'd met her at a party. You might say, I didn't even know her. But of course I did know her. We'd spent several afternoons together. But I didn't...oh God, it turned out she'd told me all sorts of lies. Almost nothing she'd told me was true. She was a fantasist. She was married. Something she'd omitted to mention. Not that I'd asked. That wasn't the nature of the venture. But still.

(NADIA is shocked, silent.)

NADIA. My God.

OLIVER. Exactly. From the bed to the roadside.

NADIA. How old was she?

OLIVER. Young. Younger than me. There was a husband, who was...lunatic. Impossible. Understandably. Wanted to sue me. A lot of stuff about the General Medical Council. But it was an accident. After all, in theory, I'd done nothing wrong.

(OLIVER is lost in thought.)

OLIVER. It was Marx, I think, who said that shame is the only revolutionary emotion. And so. I gave her everything.

NADIA. Pauline?

OLIVER. I gave her the house and every penny I had.
NADIA. You left your practice?
OLIVER. I did.
NADIA. And came here?
OLIVER. I left London. I came to live in Shropshire. I moved away to where I wouldn't do harm.

(PHILIP returns unobserved. He stops a little way off.)

OLIVER. Of course for Pauline — for Philip also — it was a simple issue. My wife had always said I was a despicable person. So at last here was the proof. She detected the workings of justice. It was what I deserved.

(OLIVER smiles, mirthless.)

OLIVER. For myself I was tired of justifying myself to another human being. I walked out. I came here to be a GP. I didn't need to. But it felt clean, it felt refreshing to stand aside from the racket. I need enough money to live, to drink decent wine, to buy books. Why do I need money to put in the bank?

(OLIVER is quiet now.)

OLIVER. To me, you see, the lesson was different. It wasn't what Philip believes. To me the lesson was: You can't spend your life in flight. Some time you have to stop running.

(OLIVER looks at her.)

OLIVER. You understand what I'm saying?

NADIA. Certainly. I think so.

OLIVER. I see life for what it is: fragile. Every moment for what it is: potentially disastrous. And, at all time, I try to take care.

(There's a silence. OLIVER has still not seen PHILIP, who speaks without moving)

PHILIP. I'm ready.

NADIA. I'll go and get my things.

PHILIP. Thank you.

(NADIA goes out. PHILIP is apprehensive.)

OLIVER. Philip. What is this? Explain to me. You're angry with me. But why? It was chance. I just happened to be sitting on the lawn.

PHILIP. In the middle of the night?

OLIVER. Yes. I was reading a book on linguistics.

(There's a silence.)

OLIVER. People are beginning to feel it may be the key to consciousness.

PHILIP. And it's coincidence, is it?

OLIVER. What's coincidence?

PHILIP. That she just happens to get up from my bed?

OLIVER. That. Yes. Coincidence.

PHILIP. And you discussed me?

OLIVER. Briefly. But not exclusively. We discussed others as well.

PHILIP. Why did you talk to her? Why did you have to talk

to her, Dad?

(OLIVER looks at him.)

OLIVER. Philip, I am not Lucifer. I don't wish you ill.
PHILIP. I didn't say you were.
OLIVER. You can spend your whole life being angry with your father. It's a waste. Truly.

(PHILIP is listening now.)

OLIVER. Who do you want to be thinking about on your deathbed?
PHILIP. I don't want to be on my deathbed.
OLIVER. No, well nor do I. Nor does anyone.
PHILIP. So?
OLIVER. In the normal sequence of things, it's a bad sign if you lie on your deathbed thinking about your father! That is not a sign of a life well lived. I would say if you're still thinking about your father, you've got real problems.
PHILIP. I won't be.
OLIVER. Good.
PHILIP. Don't flatter yourself. I won't!

(There is a moment's silence. OLIVER is quiet.)

OLIVER. You ought to plan to be thinking of her.

(PHILIP looks, only half-daring to trust him.)

OLIVER. I mean it. She's worth it.

PHILIP. All right.

OLIVER. She's worth a whole lifetime.

PHILIP. Really?

OLIVER. Yes. That's my opinion. It's my opinion. If it's of any value to you.

(PHILIP looks at him.)

PHILIP. You mean it? You really mean it?

OLIVER. Come on, she's a great woman. She's extraordinary. However, you're going to find she has what Americans call issues. She has unresolved issues. And she has some incredibly stupid ideas. But there you are. You can't have everything.

PHILIP. What sort of ideas?

OLIVER. She thinks she can set her private life away to one side. In an admirable determination to get on with things which she regards as far more important. I've tried it. It's not going to work.

PHILIP. You said that to her?

OLIVER. Of course not.

PHILIP. What did you talk about?

OLIVER. Oh…

PHILIP. Tell me.

OLIVER. Nothing much.

PHILIP. Tell me. Please. Dad.

(PHILIP nods.)

OLIVER. Your mother. Iraq. The woman I killed. Politics. Solitude. Love.

(NADIA returns, calm, humorous, fully dressed.)

NADIA. All right. I agree. We drive towards nowhere.

OLIVER. Very well.

NADIA. I'm happy. Let's do it. Let's spend the day kicking our heels and feeling remorse.

OLIVER. Have some coffee first. Let me get the stuff.

PHILIP. Dad...

OLIVER. Let me. I'd like to. At least have something before you set off.

(He goes. NADIA and PHILIP are left alone.)

NADIA. I'm sorry.

PHILIP. No. No, it's me who should be sorry. I don't know what happened. I thought he was trying to seduce you. I apologize. We can stay if you like.

(NADIA says nothing.)

PHILIP. I feel foolish.

NADIA. Don't.

(NADIA looks at him, then makes a decision.)

NADIA. I think you're right. We should go.

(They move together, and kiss. They stand holding on to each other. They look into each others' eyes. Then they part. Neither knows what to do. It's resolved, but it's not. Some moments go by.)

NADIA. Philip, I didn't mean to hurt you.

PHILIP. You didn't hurt me. Really.

(PHILIP smiles.)

NADIA. I like your father.
PHILIP. Good.

(PHILIP waits for an answer, but before she can, OLIVER returns with a tray of cups and a cafetière.)

OLIVER. Here we are. Let's have the coffee. Then I have to go and watch someone die.
PHILIP. Really? Do you have to? Why do you have to?
OLIVER. Because I said I would.
NADIA. Seems like a good reason.
OLIVER. The best.

(OLIVER fusses over the cups and saucers. A few moments go by, everyone struck by the strangeness of the situation.)

OLIVER. Anyone take sugar?

(NADIA holds up her hand. OLIVER spoons some into her cup.)

OLIVER. Philip, you always took milk.

(They smile at one another. He hands them both coffee.)

OLIVER. Good. Excellent.
(OLIVER looks out at the hills.)

OLIVER. What a splendid morning.

(The three stand, nervously drinking their coffee.)

NADIA. We'll drive carefully.
OLIVER. Please do.

Scene 9

(OLIVER, alone.)

OLIVER. I walked down the hill. I sat at my patient's bed-side all day. She was tougher than I thought. My beeper was going. But years ago I learnt: deal with one thing at a time. My patient lost life some time early that evening. I'd told her the truth and I'd stayed with her to the end. For some time, I heard nothing from Philip, nothing from Nadia. In fact, next time I read Nadia's name it was in another context entirely. When I saw what it was, forgive me, it made me smile.

Scene 10

(NADIA'S office. NADIA is once more casually dressed. Oppo-site her is TERRI SCHOLES, an African-American, just 20. She has not taken her jacket off. NADIA is holding an essay in her hand. She is passionate, disbelieving.)
NADIA. All right. I don't know. Really. I'm lost for a re-

sponse. You're an intelligent student. You're much more than that. You're a highly intelligent person. What are you actually saying? Have you thought about it? Is this what you think? Not 'I've got to do an essay, so I'd better write something'. But: 'I actually believe this. This — this is what I believe'?

(NADIA holds the essay out, quoting.)

NADIA. 'Why did Bush go to war? Because he could'. What kind of a statement is that? 'Because he knew he'd get away with it.' Do you call that a theory? 'For Bush and those like him, the exercise of power is enough in itself. America went to war for no strategic objective. Iraq was irrelevant to the war on terror and that was the reason it was chosen. The point of the action was its very arbitrariness. To demonstrate to any possible enemy of the US that no-one should ever consider themselves safe.'

(NADIA smiles and holds the pages out to TERRI.)

NADIA. Yeah, well, it's an interesting thesis, but, unburdened by evidence, maybe it doesn't quite have the impact you hope.

(NADIA waits, but TERRI is not responding.)

NADIA. I mean, Terri, I don't know, I mean, look, as a for instance, this is just a for instance, if you actually did want to prove such a thing – if you wanted to prove it – what? how – look – what shall I say? Bush walked into the Oval Office and stuck a pin in a map? He was wearing a blindfold, was he? Oh yeah? Did you see him? How would you prove it? This isn't a talk show. This isn't talk radio. It's not 'Let's go into the studio and say stupid things.' This is an essay. In a serious discipline. The causes and origins of the war in Iraq.

(NADIA shakes her head.)

NADIA. Jesus, I hear this stuff – as you do. I don't know what's happened. Suddenly everyone's a blowhard. Yale – I don't know how to put this – but the point of Yale University is – very simply - that it should be a blowhard-free zone.

(NADIA quickly corrects herself.)

NADIA. By which — look, I'm not calling you a blow-hard.
TERRI. Thanks.
NADIA. I understand there's such a thing as disaffection. I do. When you're young it's great to pretend everything is mean-ingless. It's great. Why do students all have thick curtains? So they can sit in the dark and relish the gloom. In the 19th century there was an movement in Russia called nihilism. Have you heard of it?
TERRI. Sure.
NADIA. I think you have.
TERRI. I've heard of it.
NADIA. That's the irony. Of all my students, you're one of the few who would even know what it was. But truly, they should find you an application form. Do you remember what it was they believed in?
TERRI. Nothing.

NADIA. They believed in nothing! Exactly!

TERRI. Random acts of violence.

NADIA. Right. That's what they believed in. Do you?

TERRI. No I don't. Not the violence.

NADIA. OK. Good. So just the believing-in-nothing. Terri, there's a darkness in this essay. There's a scary kind of hope-lessness. Are you going to tell me what's going on?

(There's a moment's silence.)

TERRI. All right. I'll tell you.

NADIA. Thank you.

TERRI. For a couple of weeks now, I've been breaking up with my boyfriend.

NADIA. Say what?

TERRI. My boyfriend's left me.

(NADIA frowns.)

NADIA. Well, I'm sorry. I don't know what to say. I'm sorry.

TERRI. Not as sorry as me.

(They both smile.)

NADIA. No.

TERRI. And losing him…

NADIA. Yes?

TERRI. Losing him…it's made me think hard. It's made me realize a whole heap of things.

NADIA. About American foreign policy?

TERRI. No. No, not about that. More about – more about really, how I don't want to stay on at Yale.

NADIA. Terri…

TERRI. I don't want to. Not without him.

(NADIA looks in disbelief.)

NADIA. Oh come on…

TERRI. No, I'm serious.

NADIA. I know you are. That's why I'm indignant.

TERRI. It's what I feel.

NADIA. It may be what you feel.

TERRI. It is. It is what I feel.

NADIA. I can't believe someone as gifted as you is seriously thinking of quitting solely because of some boy.

TERRI. He isn't some boy.

NADIA. No.

TERRI. He's not just some boy.

NADIA. I'm sorry.

TERRI. How would you like it if I talked about someone you knew and called him 'some boy?'

NADIA. I shouldn't have said that. I apologize.

(There's a silence.)

TERRI. I met him more or less the first day I got here.

NADIA. And?

TERRI. Just one example : every brick in this place reminds me of him.

(TERRI is a little teary, vulnerable.)

TERRI. OK, maybe it's part of the problem, I didn't bother to make other friends. I didn't need to. And some of the people I did meet didn't exactly make me want to meet any more.

NADIA. No.

TERRI. And also — I don't want to walk out on campus and see him with somebody else. So, the point of all this : I put a lot of work in that essay. It's serious. It may be the last thing I write.

(NADIA looks at her, thoughtful.)

NADIA. No, it's just – look – I'm not your counsellor…

TERRI. No…

NADIA. I'm your teacher.

TERRI. It's fine. You can't hurt me. I've been hurt enough already.

(NADIA takes another nervous, speculative look.)

NADIA. Just: I have some idea what you're going through.

TERRI. You do?

NADIA. By an interesting coincidence, this summer I broke up with someone as well.

TERRI. Why?

NADIA. Why? Well, we went on a ridiculous visit to Wales – or rather the bit beside Wales. He and I had been pretty close and yet for some reason, when I started talking with his father…I guess I began to see the son differently. Do you think that's unfair?

TERRI. Well it is unfair isn't it?

NADIA. I don't think so.

TERRI. Was his father trying to break you up?

NADIA. That's what my boyfriend believed.

TERRI. That's what I'd believe.

NADIA. Yeah. But I didn't feel that. I really don't think he was. I was only there one night. We sat out on the lawn. It was like I'd been revealed to myself.

TERRI. And what was revealed?

NADIA. I felt my own cowardice. He made me feel I'd been cowardly. In all sorts of ways. I'd made easy, cowardly choices. And also: I had this conviction — for as long as I stayed with Philip, I couldn't be true to myself.

(TERRI looks at her unconvinced.)

TERRI. Yeah, well there's a difference isn't there?

NADIA. What difference?

TERRI. You were with the wrong man.

NADIA. I don't know.

TERRI. And I was with the right one. It does make a difference.

NADIA. Yes. Yes, it's just — reading your essay, which perhaps I now begin to understand, I have this uneasy feeling that you may have been doing what psychologists call 'projecting' your unhappiness onto the subject in hand. We have to fight this, we have to make this not about ourselves, we have to fight our own feelings, we must try and be objective.

TERRI. I think I am. I'm not that stupid.

NADIA. I've never said you were stupid.

TERRI. I know we're looking at two different things. First

thing — my boyfriend has gone off with a girl who looks as if she eats shit with a dirty spoon, and also — second thing — I'm deeply despairing of the direction my government has recently been taking. I think I can hold both these things in my head at one time.

NADIA. Yes of course...

TERRI. Without confusing them!

NADIA. I'm not saying you're confusing them. All I'm saying is – look!

(Both of them have raised their voices.)

NADIA. I suppose I feel this so passionately – it's terribly important you don't simply give up.

(NADIA picks the essay up again.)

NADIA. You say here 'There is only one truth. The powerful exploit the powerless. Indiscriminately,' you say. 'And without any conscience. Rich countries are, by definition, massively self-interested and will never reach out to help anyone else. Whoever heard of a country,' you ask 'which gave up power or wealth voluntarily? Nothing ever changes except by the use of force. Reason never prevails.'

(NADIA throws it down.)

NADIA. I just ask: how can you write that?

TERRI. Because I've just lived through the last five years. I read the papers. I watch television. It's what I've seen for myself.

NADIA. You're twenty, Terri. What are you suggesting? Everything's cynicism, is it — already?

TERRI. No. But why pretend? Why argue for things which aren't going to happen? Like the world getting any more sensible?

NADIA. Because we have no other choice!

(NADIA has yelled out in anger, way beyond the demands of the situation. Realising this, she moves across the room and speaks more quietly.)

NADIA. This is what gets to me. Despair's an affectation. That's what I think. It's self-indulgence.

TERRI. I don't think so. It's more like not fooling yourself.

(NADIA looks at her, then goes and sits down at her desk.)

NADIA. I don't know. You must do what think best. Please don't do it unthinkingly. All I'm saying is: just be careful. Delay any decision.

TERRI. Well I will.

NADIA. In either context. Your studies or your private life. After all, he may come back to you.

(They both smile.)

TERRI. Thank you. Is that the end of the class?

NADIA. I guess it is.

TERRI. I'm going to give it 24 hours and then see how I feel.

NADIA. Well that's sensible. Good.

(NADIA holds out the discarded essay.)

NADIA. Take this. I don't want it.

(TERRI takes it from her and heads for the door. NADIA clicks on her desk lamp to prepare to work. Then she looks up.)

NADIA. Oh, and by the way, I should tell you if you do decide to see out your time here at Yale, I'm afraid I won't be here to see it through with you.
TERRI. Are you going to teach somewhere else?
NADIA. Not exactly. No.

(TERRI waits.)

TERRI. Are you going to tell me?
NADIA. I don't mind telling you.

(NADIA looks at her a moment.)

NADIA. I used to be a war correspondent. Recently I've noticed I miss it. I'm going back to Iraq.

END OF PLAY

Also by David Hare...

Amy's View
The Blue Room
Fanshen
Good Woman of Zetzuan
Ivanov
Judas Kiss, The
Knuckle
The Life of Galileo
A Map of the World
Mother Courage and Her Children
Plenty
Pravda
Racing Demon
The Secret Rapture
Skylight
Slag
Stuff Happens
Via Dolorosa

CPSIA information can be obtained at www.ICGtesting.com
Printed in the USA
BVOW031846270513

321652BV00010B/133/P